JESSICA WATKINS PRESENTS

I WANNA LOVE *Somebody* *Too*

I WANNA LOVE SOMEBODY PART 2

by NIQUE LUARKS

Chapter One

The end of the beginning

Blaze

"Blaze!" Kai's voice stopped my howling, but I continued to cry. I was too frightened to even look up and too petrified at the thought of glancing over at Cole's car and seeing the deadly aftermath of what looked like a murder scene. *Kenya.*

"Didn't I tell you to stay inside the club?!" He lifted me up off the ground roughly by my shoulders; yelling in my face with rage in his eyes.

Snatching away from him, I rushed to Cole's car as the passenger's side door opened.

"Blaze!" Kenya yelled out, running toward me. I made some kind of laugh-cry sound as she rushed in my direction, meeting me halfway. Her once flawless made-up face now had mascara running down her cheeks. The look in her hazel eyes was one of mortification. She began crying hysterically when she threw herself into my arms.

"Shh..." I tried to calm her down. "Calm down, Ken." I attempted to comfort her without breaking down myself, but I failed miserably. "You're okay," I choked out as tears streamed down my face. We were now holding onto each other for dear life.

"I...I thought I died." She held me tighter. "Blaze..." She trembled.

"Me too." I sniffled. "Me too." What would I do without Kenya? How could I survive through life without her craziness? My partner in crime... The thought alone had me wailing like a newborn baby. I'm sure we looked crazy holding onto each other, crying our eyes out.

"Blaze..." Kai stood next to me. "Go get in the whip."

Ignoring him, I continued to coach Kenya through her breathing. She was starting to hyperventilate. "Ken..."

"Kenya." Cole pulled her away from me. "You good, Ma. Chill." I watched as he rocked her slowly. "I got you. You straight, yo." He assured her.

"I...I could've died." Kenya's shoulders bounced as she cried into his chest.

"Man..." Cole sighed. "I ain't gon' let shit happen to your overly emotional ass. Chill." He kissed her forehead, patting her back awkwardly.

"Look at your car." She continued bawling into his chest.

"You didn't get hit with one bullet," he reminded her. "Look." He lifted her face up by her chin. "I ain't get hit neither. We good."

Kai put his phone to his ear and walked away. "Yo, meet me at the spot," he roared angrily.

"Kenya." I directed my attention back to Cole and a distressed Kenya.

She sniffled.

"Where's my gangster?" He rested his chin on the top of her head.

Cole

I was so mad that I could feel my blood boiling in my veins. Kenya crying in my arms had me ready to paint the city red. She was real-life boo-hooing. Snot and all. Holding onto me like if she let me go she'd lose me forever. This was the second time she'd cried in my arms like this. The only difference this time was that her heart wasn't broken. My little gangster was scared.

I'd been bullet proofing my cars for the past three years. Niggas wouldn't catch me slippin'; not even on my worst days. I had too much to lose, especially with Tati riding shotgun all the time.

"Kenya." Blaze rubbed her arm. "Calm down, okay. We can go back to Jersey and catch a flight back to Kansas City in a couple of hours." She wiped her own face.

Leave? Kenya wasn't leaving New York; at least not today.

"Blaze, what the fuck did I say?!" Kai came out of nowhere, looking down on Blaze. She gave him a puzzled look. "Go get your hard-headed ass in the car," he said a little calmer, but his voice still held an authoritative tone.

Aw shit. I watched as her lip quivered. These cry babies were about to stress a nigga out. It looked like she wanted to say something slick. Instead, she spun on her heels and stomped to Kai's whip. He followed, cursing under his breath.

"Kenya." I slowly inhaled, then exhaled deeply. "I'ma take care of it." I led her toward Kai's whip. Hopping in the back, I pulled her close to me as I shut the door.

"We on the way now. Yeah...one." Kai hung up his phone and started the ignition.

"Are you taking us back to Jersey?" Blaze sniffled.

4

"Why are you crying, Blaze?" he asked, speeding out of the parking lot. Taking a deep breath, he sighed and shook his head. "Stop crying." His voice softened.

Ole pussy-whipped ass. I smirked wrapping my arm around Kenya.

"Leave me alone, Mehkai," she snapped.

"Man..." He leaned back in his seat. "Yeah...a'ight."

"Are you taking us back to Jersey?" she pressed.

Hell nah. I almost answered, but Kai had it covered.

"Nah. I'ma drop you off and you gon' chill for a second. A'ight?" He asked her for her okay, but I already knew she had no other choice.

"You can just take us back to the hotel." I chuckled. Let me find out Giggles got heart.

"What did I say? Sit back and put your seatbelt on." Kai ignored her temper tantrum, speeding through a red light.

Kenya

I've never been so scared in all my twenty-five years of living. I was sure my life was over with each bullet that

5

struck Cole's car. It was like he'd seen the shooters before they even started shooting. He pushed me on the floor right before a barricade of bullets began rocking his car. Yeah, I was positive I'd died. Then the gunshots stopped and I was still alive.

I held onto Cole as Kai sped through the half-filled New York streets. *These people really don't sleep.* The twenty-minute car ride was a silent one. Nothing could be heard besides the sound of Blaze sniffling every once in a while. I knew she was just as shaken up as I was. She was my other half; I'm sure the incident had her emotions everywhere as well.

Kai came to a stop in front of a skyscraper and parked the car. Cole opened his door. "Come on." He gestured for me to get out of the car.

Following his orders, I slid across the seat as he grabbed my hand and helped me out. As he shut the door, Kai opened Blaze's door.

"Come on, Ma." He sighed, running his left hand down his face.

"I said I wanted to go back to Jersey. Shut my door please," Blaze replied; her voice laced with irritation.

"Man..." He reached into the car and pulled her out honeymoon style.

Even though I was upset, I tried to stifle my laughter as I watched Blaze cross her arms. Kai shut the door with his foot, and we followed him into the immaculate glass building that I would later learn he called home.

Kai

I made my way through the doors of my condo's lobby, stood at the elevator, and even unlocked and opened my front door with a pouting Blaze in my arms. I continued to my room leaving Cole and Kenya in the living room. Blaze's stubborn ass kept her arms folded the whole time. Once I made it up the stairs and into the master suite, I shut the door with my right elbow. Carrying her cry-baby ass to my bed, I laid her down.

Resting on my palms, I hovered over her, looking into her sad eyes. My baby was a wreck. Somebody was about to pay in blood.

"Blaze." She turned her head. Kissing her neck, I positioned myself between her legs. She continued to play mad as I licked and sucked on her neck and collar bone.

"Why you mad at me?" I wanted to know...*needed* to know. I mean yeah, a nigga had snapped on her, but that was because she wasn't listening to me. The sooner Blaze learned I'd always have her best interest, the better off we'd be.

Still, she ignored me.

Roughly lifting her dress up over her ass, I continued to attack the sensitive spots on her sweet neck. Slowly sliding the tight material over her perky breasts, then over her head, I exposed her beautiful naked body. My dick bricked immediately as my eyes roamed across her pierced nipples, flat stomach, and pretty pussy.

"I'm sorry," I apologized before stealing a kiss. "I didn't mean to come at you like that, Ma. You need to listen to me when I tell you to do something." I made her look at me. "If anything would've happened to you tonight, I would've lost it." I kissed her again. "Can you picture me in a straitjacket?"

It might've come out like a joke, but I was speaking from my heart; something I only did for Blaze. I felt her body loosen up underneath me.

"You forgive me?" I asked, looking into her eyes for my answer. Again she ignored me. "Baby..." I whispered into the crook of her neck as I unzipped my jeans.

Releasing my dick from my briefs, I slid the head down her opening. I made sure to take my time as I entered her love. Blaze might've looked mad, but her pussy was singing a different tune.

"Mmm..." she moaned softly as I planted my lips on hers.

"I'm sorry," I found myself apologizing again.

"Kai..." she whined, wrapping her hands around my neck.

"Yeah, baby?" I kissed her hungrily sucking on her bottom lip.

"Uhhh..." she replied as I grabbed her waist with my right hand, resting my left arm above her head.

Grinding slowly, I enjoyed the warm feeling of Blaze's juices running down my nuts. I watched as her pupils rolled to the back of her head before she closed her eyes. Every time I deep stroked her, she let out a sexy whimper.

"You forgive me, baby?" I licked her earlobe.

"Baby..." she moaned out as her body became stiff.

I pressed my lips hard on hers to quiet her moaning.

"Oh my God!" she cried out into my mouth. "Kai!"

"You gon' start listening to Daddy, Blaze?" I bit down on her bottom lip, going harder.

"Yes...yes, baby." She let out a bated breath, trying to push me back by my hips. "Kai...wait...that's my spot." She tried to run from a second orgasm but failed.

"Aaaaagghh! Shit!" she screamed as I sped up. "Kai, I'm cumming." I kissed her face and she released again. "Kai..." she whispered.

Unable to hold back any longer, I pulled out and came on her stomach. "Fuck,"
I huffed out of breath.

"Yo, Kai, we need to head out, son." Cole knocked on the door.

My voice was stuck in my throat, so all I could manage was a grunt, which I'm sure he didn't hear. Blaze looked spent as I removed all my clothes and headed to the bathroom to run us a hot shower.

10

Chapter Two

What now

Blaze

I watched Kai get dressed as I laid in his bed in one of his white T-shirts. He slipped his feet into his black Timberlands and then reached for the black hoodie sitting on the bed. Pulling it over his head, he adjusted it to fit to his liking before he looked over at me.

"It's a fridge full of food," he told me, standing up.

"Where are you going?" I pried.

"Out. So don't wait up. Go to sleep, go check on sis, and cook something." He hovered over me, planting a soft kiss on my forehead.

"I have to work in the morning, Mehkai. I can't stay here."

He frowned. "Call in."

"I can't." My reputation was on the line.

"Blaze..."

"Mehka..."

"Stay until I get back, a'ight? I'll take you back to Jersey."

I huffed. "Are you going to be back by ten?"

"Yeah, I should be." He shrugged.

"Those are two different answers. Are you going to be back or no?" I crossed my arms.

He chuckled. "Yeah. So don't leave this muthafucka." He pecked me quickly on the lips before standing up.

My eyes stayed on him as he went into one of his many dresser drawers. He dug through it for a second and then closed it. Holding a black ski mask in his hands, he eyed me as he rested it on top of his head.

What the hell? I looked over his attire. Kai looked like he was about to rob a bank or commit some other crime. He usually sported some kind of jewelry, but he had none on. Not even his diamond studs.

"I'll be back." He winked and then left me.

***

"So you think they're going to go find the niggas that shot Cole's car up?" Kenya asked before taking a sip of the steaming, peach tea I'd found in Mehkai's cabinets.

"I mean you saw Kai before he left. He had a damn ski mask on his head." I shook my head.

"So, you think they've killed people before?"

"Kenya, I don't know. I just don't want anything to happen to him or Cole." She sighed. "What if they don't make it back?"

"Blaze, quit." She smacked her lips. "Don't burn bread on them. All we can do is pray."

I frowned. "Kenya, this is *real life*. You could've died tonight," I reminded her.

She scoffed. "You don't think I know that?" Annoyance was written all over her face.

"Then stop acting like this is normal because it's not! *This* is not a normal conversation, Ken." I could feel myself getting angry. Kenya read too many books. It was as if her near-death experience tonight no longer phased her.

"Look." She put her mug down. "Stop talking to me like I'm slow. Blaze, I know I could've died. You didn't think I was scared?" She paused. "But at the same time, this is the lifestyle Cole and Kai live. Hell, Kai *just* got out of prison. He ain't even been out a full year yet."

"What's your point, Kenya?"

"'My point, *Blaze*, is you knew Kai was in the streets before you started fucking him.

We both sat silent. As much as I hated to admit it, Kenya was right. I'd bumped into Kai at his homecoming party just a couple months ago. Hell, the man had two teardrops under his right eye. Kai was a gangster from the way he talked to the way he walked. Anyone could look into his eyes and see he was a force to be reckoned with.

Finally breaking the awkward silence, Kenya sighed. "I can't believe the night turned out like this."

"Me either. I was so scared you were gone, Ken." My eyes began to water.

"Girl...*you*? I was sure if those bullets didn't kill me, I was going to die of a heart attack." She chuckled. "Cole said he bulletproofs all his cars...says cats in New York aren't really feeling him."

"Mmm..."

"He also said he and Kai will handle it and that we have nothing to worry about." She shrugged. "And I believe him."

"So you don't care about the lifestyle he lives? It doesn't bother you? Scare you?"

How was Kenya so calm about the whole situation? When it first happened, I could barely get her to breathe on her own. Now, she was sitting here trying to convince me I was the one overreacting. She was vouching for Cole and Mehkai's criminal asses like she was some kind of seasoned mob wife.

"Blaze—"

"Kenya, let's just not even debate about it. We're not going to come to a mutual agreement."

"So, just like that you're done with Kai?" she questioned, raising the mug to her lips again. "After gave the coochie up and everything."

My eyes almost popped out of their sockets. "What?!" I quickly denied her accusations. "I don't know what—"

"Bitch, please." She laughed after taking a quick sip. "*Ooooh, Kai!*" she started moaning.
And my cheeks caught fire. "*I love you,*" she continued moaning loud, attempting to mock me.

"Oh my God." I hung my head in shame.

"Uh uh!" She playfully hit my forearm. "Don't play coy now, hoe. I saw you in that VIP." She cracked up laughing at my expense.

Oh my God.

"Umhm!" I came to tell you we were about to try to hit up another club. Imagine my surprise when I pulled back the curtain and saw you throwing it back like a pro." She beamed proudly. Raising the cup, she saluted me. "I taught you well, grasshopper."

A laugh escaped my lips. "You're stupid." I shook my head, embarrassed.

"I would ask how it was, but your face told it all." Her mouth fell agape and she rolled her eyes to the back of her head.

By now, I was holding onto my stomach, almost unable to breathe from laughing. She gave a hearty laugh as well, throwing her head back.

"He..." she tried to speak through laughter. "He had to have put it down." She paused, giving me a smug look. "He carried your ass up them stairs and y'all disappeared for thirty minutes. Now, you're sitting here in nothing but his T-shirt with that I-just-got-some-good-dick afterglow."

I snickered.

She pouted. "I'm jealous."

"And for your information, I never said *I love you*. So, don't try to play me."

She rolled her eyes. "But answer my question."

16

"What question?" I asked dumbfounded.

"Are...you...done...with...Kai?" she asked slowly like I had comprehension issues.

Was I through with Mehkai? Could I walk away from him just like that? Kenya eyed me waiting patiently on an answer I didn't have. Walk away from Kai forever? My stomach churned from even considering it.

"I-I don't know," I finally answered honestly.

She nodded her head in understanding. "I get it." She sighed. "I know deep in my heart that Cole ain't no good for me," she mumbled sadly.

"What are we going to do?" I asked rhetorically. We were both in deep with two men tied to the streets.

"I don't know about you," She cleared her throat. "But I'm just going with the flow. I like Cole. He's cool," she admitted. "The entire time his car was getting shot up, he held me, telling me everything was going to be al right. *He had me.* "She chortled. "Of course I didn't believe his ass." She looked off. "I trusted him."

"Wow!"

"What?" She looked at me.

"Y'all are like the two thousand and seventeen Bonnie and Clyde." I grinned and she did too.

"Whatever, fool." She snickered, standing up.

***

"Blaze, some chick is banging on the front door hollering Kai's name."

Kenya had barged into Mehkai's room no less than sixty seconds ago, jolting me out of my sleep. That's why I was currently looking through the peephole at Monique. She had a silk Gucci scarf wrapped around her head and a mean scowl etched on her face. I sighed as she lifted her fist to bang on the door again.

"Kai! Open this fuckin' door!" She hollered.

"Who the fuck is she?" Kenya asked with an attitude.

"That's Monique. Kai's..." Shit, I honestly didn't know *who* Monique was to Mehkai. She claimed to be his woman, but the way he'd handled her earlier gave me reasons to doubt that.

"The bitch better get on." Kenya seethed, taking my position in front of the door. "Get the fuck away from this door!" she yelled, looking through the peephole.

"Oh hell no!" Monique screeched. "Kai!" The banging became louder. The frame even shook a little.

"This crazy broad is kicking the door." Kenya chuckled. "I'ma have fun whooping her tough ass."

I frowned. "Uh...no. Monique can be crazy out there. We're not stooping down to her level, Kenya. I don't want to go to jail in New York," I huffed.

Monique continued to try and kick the door off its hinges. "I'ma beat that bitch ass on God!" she screamed. "Blaze, on my dead family, I'm beating your ass."

I inhaled slowly, counting back from ten.

"What?! Bitch, ain't no hoe in our blood." Kenya started to pop the locks on the door, but I quickly stopped her.

Blaze be the bigger, more mature person. Don't give this irrelevant bitch control over your emotions, I began to talk myself out of opening the door.

"Kenya." I pulled her away from the door.

"Bring your scary ass out!" Monique wouldn't let up.

"Monique, go home. Mehkai isn't here." I could feel my blood pressure rising.

She kicked the door again.

"Blaze!" Kenya was having a hard time keeping her cool. "Just open the door and let the bitch in and lock her in. We can tag team her ignorant ass."

I shook my head no.

"Ma'am," a male's voice called out from the other side of the door.

"What?!"

"I'm going to have to ask you to leave the building or I'll have to call the police on you," he warned calmly.

"I don't give a fuck!" she spat. "Call 'em."

"She really tryna punk you." Kenya shook her head violently. "This trick just ain't knowing."

"Ma'am, if you don't exit this building right now, I'll have no choice but to alert the authorities. You're disturbing the peace," he warned her again.

"You know what? I'ma catch you, bitch, so don't even trip," she threatened before hitting the door one last time. Then I heard footsteps as she walked away.

"Blaze, you're better than me." Kenya paced back and forth angrily.

"We're leaving." I headed toward the gorgeous wraparound stairs.

"What?"

"Get all your shit together. I'm calling an Uber or a cab or *something*," I spoke, making my way up the stairs.

"Why?"

"Because if she comes back, I'm going to jail."

I needed to get as far away from anything or anyone that had *something* to do with Kai. His life was just too chaotic for me. I had a career and my dignity to protect. I couldn't and I wouldn't allow his drama-filled life to knock me off my square or distract me.

Was I done with Kai? Yes! Yes, I was.

Chapter Three

Murder, Murder

Cole

"Cole, man, don't do this. I got kids." Dre's cries bounced off the walls of the empty warehouse. "I got shorties, man." His tear-stained face looked pathetic, as snot bubbles hung from his nose.

"Fuck yo kids!" My own voice echoed throughout the building. I didn't give one fuck.

He cried louder.

"Shut that bitch shit up." Kai gave an irritated sigh.

"What y'all want? Money? They got that. Let me go and I can get you some paper. Tell me what y'all want .I'll get it. Just don't kill me." His pleading eyes bounced back and forth between me and Kai.

I snatched my burner from my waist and pointed it at his head.

"Who is *they*?" Kai asked calmly.

"Fuck all that!" I yelled. I wasn't tryna hear nothing else the nigga had to say. Pulling the trigger twice, I put one in his head and one in his chest before he hit the concrete floor.

"This nigga..." Nasir snickered behind me.

"Yo, Cole, I get that you mad and all, but you need to chill the fuck out." Kai stepped next to me, looking down at Dre.

"Fuck him."

"Cole's trigger-happy ass done murked the nigga before we could get a fuckin' lead." Quan bent down next to Dre's lifeless body and started digging in his pockets.

"Point." Nasir cosigned.

"Man, fuck y'all too. Y'all ain't seen the damage them niggas did to my whip," I said, tucking my heat into my waist band at the small of my back. "I just got that fuckin' ride."

Quan stood up holding Dre's wallet and cell. "So what now?"

"What you mean *what now*?" Nasir crossed his arms over his chest. "Niggas is obviously looking for war, so I say we give 'em one, son."

I nodded in agreement. That's why I fucked with Nasir the long way. We were a lot alike. Both of us were considered hot-headed and ruthless than a muthafucka. If niggas wanted me dead, then I'd gladly return the favor. I could get down with a war.

"The fuck outta here." Quan scoffed stuffing his pockets with cash from Dre's wallet. "Who y'all niggas goin' to war with? New York?"

Kai chuckled.

Quan was a smart but reckless nigga from Queens; him and Nasir. He had graduated at the top of his class and shit. He had ended up going to college to be a doctor or some shit like that. But then he dropped out when his mother died. He and Nasir ran Queens together before Kai put 'em on.

Unlike Kai, who had known Nasir before he went to prison, they were both new to me. I couldn't front and say the niggas didn't put in mad work, though, because they held shit down. We were moving major dope and heavy artillery throughout the east coast and all through the Midwest, and down south. Kai had some heavy connects with these Jamaicans and some kingpin nigga named Tone. At twenty-eight, we were wealthy...fuck *rich*. Our kids' kids would be able to eat off the paper we were making. Our pocket change held more value than a doctor's salary.

Nasir fired up a blunt just as Dre's phone started ringing in Quan's hands. Answering, he put it on speaker phone and handed it over to Kai.

"Yo, Dre! That nigga, Cole, ain't dead. You and Joey need to meet me *now*!" a husky voice boomed from the phone's speaker.

"Fuck you!" I roared, enraged that the nigga who wanted me dead was on the other end of the receiver, but I couldn't get to him.

"Hello? Who is this?" he asked.

Kai put his hand up, reminding me to chill. "You want Cole dead? Why?" he asked, looking directly at me.

"Where is Dre? Joey?" the guy on the other end questioned. "Where is my son?"

Instead of answering, Kai ended the call.

"What the fuck you hang up for?" I grilled him, stepping in his face. Niggas was tryna murder me. No niggas was about to make me his target and I do nothing about it. Kai had me fucked up.

Quan and Nasir quickly stepped between us. "Chill." Quan spoke up.

Kai placed the burner phone in his back pocket. "Yo, Cole, I get that you got ill feelings, but I ain't the one, my nigga." His jaws clenched as he stared me down.

We stood mugging each other and Nasir sucked his teeth. "Y'all done?"

"Get with the cleanup crew," Kai ordered, still flexing.

"A'ight," Quan said. "You niggas good?" he asked, still trying to keep the peace.

Nasir, still puffing on his blunt, took a hit and tapped my arm. "Here." He tried handing it to me.

"Nah. I need to know why you hung up."

I was New York born and bred. I'd been around scandalous niggas my whole life. Kai hanging up on dude before we could get any answers had my antennas up. The fuck was he on? Everything in me wanted to draw my burner on him.

"You think he was 'bout to tell me who he was?" Kai frowned. "He unintentionally gave us info, and that's all that matters."

I stood my ground.

"What? You wanna shoot me?" He smirked.

Is this nigga trying to pull my hoe card? I reached for my gun, placed it in front of me and crossed my wrist.

Kai chuckled.

"Ayo, Cole, you trippin'." Quan shook his head in disbelief, stepping back.

Yeah, nigga, that's your best bet.

"Yo, Cole..." Kai started, eyeballing me. "You acting like a real bitch right now."

Kai

Cole was letting his emotions get the best of him. Technically, he hadn't pulled his gun out on me, but I could look in his eyes and tell his trigger finger was itchin' something serious. I wanted these niggas just as bad as he did. I didn't like chaos. It was too much of a distraction from what was important—*money.*

Yeah, his car had gotten shot up, but this was nothing new. Only difference was Kenya got caught in the crossfire. Shit...maybe that's why he was trippin' hard like this. He was so deep in his feelings, it hadn't registered we were winning right now. Dre was dead. And whoever Joey was, he was next.

The only real pressing issue was Cole and his temper tantrum he was currently throwing. I was more pissed about that, than the gun he was waving around.

27

"Nasir, find Joey." I continued my stare down with Cole. "Quan, track down the number that just called."

They hesitated, probably debating whether or not they should leave or stay just in case they needed to break up a fight. Cole wouldn't shoot me. He was a lot of things, but dumb wasn't one of them.

"A'ight. I'll hit yo' line when I find the nigga." Nasir stepped over Dre's body. I had no doubt he would find this Joey cat and deliver him to me. Nasir knew everybody. He was on the block even when he didn't have to be. People feared him yet respected him at the same time.
Quan gave an unsure look before he took off after Nasir and out of the warehouse.

"Tell me something, nigga," Cole grilled me, gun still in hand and his wrists still crossed. If he was anybody else I would've had Nasir kill him before he even had the opportunity to reach for his banger. But Cole was my ace. I'd let him get this one off. One.

"Once Nasir finds Joey and Quan traces that call, we'll kill everybody involved." That's the only explanation I was willing to offer. The rest should've been common sense.

He let what I said register, looked down at Dre, and shook his head. A menacing grin slowly spread across his face as he tucked his gun.

"Yo, Kai, I'ma hold you to that," he stated, fixing his hoodie.

I nodded as the garage doors to the warehouse opened and a black 1999 Honda Civic pulled in.

Right on time

I waited for the cleanup crew to handle Dre's body. They would dispose of it properly. I could count on it.

"Sup, Boss?" Rico, a young nigga from Harlem, approached us. "What we got here?" He looked down at the body and shook his head. "Damn, Dre."

I looked on in silence as he and a few other cats dragged the body to the trunk. Dre had only been down with the team for about two months. When I ran outside the strip joint bustin' at the black Ford Explorer that was lightin' Cole's car up, I peeped him duck his head quickly back inside the SUV. All I had to do was have Nasir and Quan pick him up from his baby mama house and bring him here. It was good we'd gotten rid of him because he was messy. His death being proof. What type of nigga in his right mind shoots up a strip joint bare faced?

He made finding him *and* catching him way too easy. I couldn't afford those kind of slip ups in my camp. One person's fuck up could be all of our downfall. I had too much at stake. His death would be used as a lesson.

"Yo, Dre, keep his head."

Chapter Four

Forward

Kenya

I was sleeping oh so good when the loud banging on my front door jolted me out of my deep slumber. *Who the hell?* I reached for my phone next to me, squinting my eyes as the screen lit up. No missed calls or texts. Sitting up slowly, I stretched, yawned and flopped back down onto my queen size bed. Maybe if I ignored the knocking, whoever it was would go away.

I just wanted to sleep. Between working, flying back and forth from New York, and sexing Cole, I was beat. The days weren't long enough it seemed and my work load was piling up. Our human resource department was going through layoffs so I was stuck doing interviews until told otherwise. My love life and my career were booming, but I was tired as hell. And just when I thought the person banging on my door would get the hint and go away, their ignorant ass started banging harder.

I'm about to curse somebody the fuck out. I huffed, lifting up and off my plush bed. I took my time, but frowned the whole way down to the door. Blaze and my mother had keys, so I assumed it was my sister, Amina.

"Who is it!?" I asked, ready to snatch the door open and smack whoever was standing on the other side.

"Jamarcus."

I smacked my lips, pressed my forehead against the door, and sighed. I hadn't spoken to him since his pop up at my job. Call me naïve, but I honestly thought after that conversation, I was officially rid of Jamarcus and his bullshit.

"Kenya, open the door please. I need to talk to you and get the rest of my shit." He had the nerve to sound like he had an attitude, which made me catch one instantly.

Snatching the door open, I came face to face with my first everything and my biggest regret. "You didn't leave shit here. I took everything to your moms." I rolled my eyes. We'd been broken up for months. *Months.* He didn't have shit here. The only man who had clothes and shoes here was Cole with his shopaholic ass.

"I got some shit bagged up in the upstairs hall closet." His eyes quickly washed over me in wonderment. "Who in there? Why can't I come in?" He tried to look past me.

"Nobody, and because I don't fuck with you like that, Jamarcus. If you left something here, I'll take it to your mom's house or sister's tomorrow." I started to shut the door.

"I need it tonight. I'm leaving for New York in the morning."

"New York?" My eyebrow shot up.

"Yeah. My cousin, Kai that just got out of prison got some work for me to do up there, so I'ma go see what he talkin' about." He shrugged.

"What kind of work?" It was none of my business and it hadn't even registered that Kai was his cousin who had just gotten out of jail until Blaze told me a little while ago, but what work was Jamarcus talkin' about? I couldn't see Cole or Kai working with somebody as shiesty as him.

"He said he needs some muscle, so I'ma check it out."

Nigga, you don't even have no muscles. I looked him up and down, annoyed.

"So can I come in? It's cold out here. I promise I won't stay that long." The cold wind reminded me it was freezing outside and my heat was on.

"You got five minutes to get all of your shit and go. Whatever you leave behind today, I'm taking to the Salvation Army tomorrow."

He shook his head as I stepped to the side and let him in. "Why you so damn evil?" he asked as I shut the door.

"Your time is ticking." I folded my arms across my chest and nodded to the top of the stairs.

"Man..." He sighed, but started taking the stairs two at time.

Going into my living room, it was pitch black, so I turned on the lamps on my end tables. Taking a seat on my love seat, I placed my face in my hands and sighed. I couldn't wait for him to

33

leave so I could go back to sleep. *I should've given him two minutes as a matter of fact*

I stood up and headed toward the staircase. Stopping at the bottom, I leaned over on the railing. "Times up." When he didn't say anything and I didn't hear any movement, I started up the steps. "Jamarcus, you need to leave."

Reaching the top of the stairs, I looked in the direction of the hall closet where he said his shit was and immediately became irritated when I saw he wasn't there. I was about to call out to him again when I heard a small thud come from my bedroom. "See, this is why you can't be nice to niggas." I sighed. Just as I stepped in my room, he was coming out of my closet.

"Whose shit is that hanging up?" he grilled me. "You got a nigga living here already?"

I frowned. "For one, why are you in my room? You said you had shit in the hall closet and not in mine." I rolled my eyes. "Did you find what you were looking for so you can go?"

"So that's why it's so easy for you to just give up on us." He eyed me, shaking his head in disbelief. "'Cause you bouncing from dick to dick." He inched closer toward me.

"Whatever, Jamarcus, your five minutes is up. Whatever you forget after you leave ain't yours no more, so I hope while your nosy ass was all in my shit, you took everything that belongs to you."

"*You* belong to me." His crazy ass said with a straight face.

"No, I don't."

"Since when?"

"Are you slow? You're the reason we aren't together. 'Cause you couldn't keep your dick in your pants. Don't come back months later questioning me and acting all crazy."

"I'ma kill that nigga." His nostrils flared. "I swear to God."

I waved his dramatic ass off. "You ain't killing shit." I would've actually believed his threat had it come from somebody else, but Jamarcus wasn't even built like that.

"Oh, so now I'ma *bitch*?"

I chuckled. "Are we done here?"

"What's his name?"

"Why?!"

He was starting to piss me off.

"You love him?"

"Jamarcus…"

"You love him?"

Not that it was any of his business, but if it would make him leave. I shrugged. "I think so."

"Wow." He shook his head. "I bet he a broke-ass nigga too."

I smirked. "Takes one to know one." I'm sure while he was in my closet lurking, he saw all the expensive shoes and clothes. Cole had shit with tags still on them. Five hundred dollar Gucci belts, nine hundred dollar shirts and shit. Not to mention all the new shoes and purses he'd bought me. I had shit I would probably never get to wear twice.

"Ain't shit about me broke."

I stepped to the side so he could get past me. Instead, he stopped directly in front of me and looked down. "I'm going to New York to get my money up. I know I fucked up, Kenya. I fell off hard." He gripped my chin. "But I'ma fix us. I'm not giving up on you. I love you."

I pulled away. "There isn't anything to fix, Jamarcus. I already told you. What's done is done. Let it go. Let me go."

"I can't." He shook his head. "I got some Crip homies up there, so even if shit with Kai don't work out, I'll be straight."

"The same Crip homie you were fuckin' and got caught with?" I hadn't forgotten about that hoe, Destiny, a wanna-be gang-bangin' bitch he seemed to have had a hard time letting go of.

"I'ma show you, Kenya." He finally walked past me and proceeded to descend down the stairs. I heard the front door open and close, letting me know he was gone.

Four days later...

Cole

"You're cheating," Kenya pouted as I knocked the eight ball in.

"Nah, yo ass just can't play."

"Well, you could've at least let me win." She went to set the game back up. "That's usually how dates work. Be a gentleman sometimes." She laughed.

"I don't need to be a gentleman. I'm the realist nigga you know." I smirked and she rolled those pretty hazel eyes.

"Being a *real nigga* is so high school, though." She shrugged. "Being a *man* is sexy."

"I'm *both*."

"How can you be both?" she questioned, finally setting the game back up. Taking a seat on the corner of the table, she waited for my answer.

"I'm a real nigga 'cause I demand respect, do whatever necessary to get bread, and make sure my family is eating."

"Ain't that what a man does?"

"If you would let me finish, I could break it down for yo know-it-all ass." I licked my lips when she tilted her head to the side with fire in her eyes. She was itchin' to say some slick shit, but she sighed instead. I eyed her little feisty ass until she looked away shyly.

"Okay, are you going to tell me or stare at me all night?" she asked with an attitude, looking down at her hands and playing with her nails.

"I'ma do both." Kenya's little ass was gon' make me hem her up. "I'm a man because I make sacrifices for the people I love. I say I'm both because all I knew growing up and hugging the block was to be a real nigga. Being a man and making sacrifices wasn't something I was interested in. Growing up with my mother on drugs and not knowing who my father was; I guess you can say molded me into feeling like it was me against the world. I didn't give a fuck about nobody or nothing. And honestly, I'm still learning how to give a fuck the right way."

She finally looked up at me. "So what made you want to be a man?" Her eyes danced around my face. "Why the change of heart?"

"My daughter was born."

She smiled.

"The first time I ever held her and shit I knew right then and there I would lay my life on the line for her. I stopped going out as much. I started making better and smarter decisions. I finally had something to live for, somebody who depended on me." Tatianna was a soft spot for me, so talking to Kenya about her started making me feel uncomfortable. Open.

"Can I ask you something?"

I shrugged just as Lyfe Jennings' "Must Be Nice" started bumping throughout the bar.

"Have you ever had a best friend?"

I frowned. "Yo, I'm grown as fuck. What the fuck I look like having a best friend?"

She laughed hopping off the table. "I have a best friend." She walked closer to me.

"And?"

"And I just so happen to have room for another one."

"What that gotta do wit' me?"

She rolled those eyes again. Sexy ass... "Why you gotta be so damn rude?" She shook her head, reaching for her pool stick again. "I'm just saying that relationships between men and women flourish when they feel comfortable enough to be themselves. No holding back." Her eyes landed on mine. "One day you're going to beg and I mean *beg* me to marry you."

I chuckled.

In true Kenya fashion, she continued. "But before we get to that point, I want to know everything about you. And I want you to know everything about me. I don't want you to shut me out. I get that you're a real nigga, and to be for real, that's what drew me to you. But that look you had in your eyes when you were just talkin' about being a father to your daughter was sexy as hell." She licked her plump, shiny lips and gave me a seductive look. "That's the Cole I wanna get to know...Cole the man."

"Yo, you wild."

"No, I'm serious."

Chapter Five

I'm ready for love

Blaze

I laid across my king size bed thinking. It had been two weeks since me and Kenya had left Mehkai's condo in New York, and I hadn't spoken to him. Not one phone call or a simple text. *Nothing.*

I huffed, irritated at my conflicted feelings. The moment I left his home, it was like a ton of bricks were placed on my chest. I didn't want to leave, but I had to for my sanity.

What if he's mad at me? Maybe that's why I hadn't heard from him. I knew he was alive and well because every time I talked to Kenya, she had some funny story about something Cole did or said.

Flipping over on my stomach, I reached for my phone. Going into my contacts, I looked at his name. My index finger hovered over the screen. *What if he doesn't answer?*

Sighing, I closed my eyes. "Just call the man, Blaze. You at least owe him an explanation." It wasn't his fault Monique decided to show up unannounced.

I began doubting my own actions. Maybe I'd overreacted. I could've at least called and let him know I was safe. Plus we'd rushed out and left his front door unlocked. Anybody could've walked in. Monique could've come back and vandalized his home.

I looked down at my phone again. *I should call.* He was probably worried. I let my last conclusion marinate, but then instantly became annoyed. He couldn't have been worried about me. Like I said, he hadn't reached out to me. Not once. Kenya had told me she told Cole about Monique's pop up. So he *knew* why I'd left. Still nothing.

Humph. I tapped on his name and put the phone on speaker. It rang a few times before he answered.

"Yeah ..."

Yeah? I frowned at the phone, taken back by how brash he'd come off.

"What do you want, Blaze?" he asked coldly.

In that very moment, I was positive the bricks that weighed heavy on my heart, broke it in half. My sole purpose for calling was to check him for not reaching out to me. Maybe even apologize for storming out the way I had. However, his tone had completely thrown me for a loop.

"Why are you talking to me like that?" I damn near whispered.

"Like what? Why does it matter how I talk to you? You stopped fucking with the kid. Not the other way around." He scoffed. "I ain't about to chase you, Blaze. You're dope don't get me wrong. Ill as fuck. I'm diggin' the shit outta you, Ma."He paused. "You're a great person. Beautiful."

Even though he was chastising me, I gushed at how highly he spoke of me.

"Any nigga would be lucky to wife you. Have you in his corner."

"Kai..."

"Apparently, I ain't that nigga." He cut me off and continued. "My life is too fast-paced for you lil mama. I got too much shit going on to be worried about you running out on a nigga every time you get mad."

"I wasn't—"

"And I'm too fuckin' grown to play high school games with you," he interrupted again. "I ain't no perfect nigga, Blaze, but shit, I know my worth too, shorty. I been real with you from the jump."

The line then fell silent.

"Can I get a word in?"

He said nothing.

"Kai, I like you a lot, but I told you I thought it would be best if we were just friends," I reminded him.

Silence.

"I did." I became defensive. "I told you it would be better that way.

"Better for who? *You*?" He chuckled lightly. "Yo, Blaze, if that's what you want, a'ight. Again, what do you want?" His icy tone was breaking me down.

"I wanted to call and explain to you why I just up and left."

"After I told you not to..." he stated.

I rolled my eyes. "Monique came over acting a fool."

"I know."

"Mehkai, I have too much riding on my career to jeopardize it now."

"Okay," he said dryly.

"*Okay*?"

"Yo, you confused as fuck, Ma. The fuck you want me to say, Blaze?"

I didn't know the answer to that question.

He sighed. "Look—"

"No, Mehkai, you look." My feelings were officially hurt. "I care about you, but how do you expect me to act or be, after my best friend got caught up in a fucking shootout? You left in a ski mask, and the bitch you're fucking with showed up to your door acting like a damn lunatic! I was upset, Mehkai." My breathing became labored. "I-I'm...I'm scared to love you."

There. I said it. I, Blaze Monroe Santiago, was terrified of falling in love with a man like Mehkai. The idea of giving my all to him paralyzed me.

"I don't want you to be scared of me." His voice softened but only a little.

"I am. I can't give you that much control over my emotions. We're not even serious and look how you have me acting."

"Who says we ain't serious?" He grunted and hung up the phone.

Shocked, I sat my phone down next to me. Laying down, I placed my head between my folded arms and closed my eyes. A sea of different emotions washed over me. Relief. Sadness. Regret. *Desire*. I didn't realize I was on the verge of tears until my phone alerted me of an incoming FaceTime and I had to open my eyes.

Mehkai's name flashed across my screen. Pressing the green icon, I answered. His face appeared with a scowl, but softened as he gazed at me. We sat silently looking at one another for all of two minutes. Finally, he ran his free hand down his face, sighing seemingly in frustration.

"Why are you running from me, Blaze?"

"I don't want to give you the power to hurt me," I confessed.

"I thought you trusted me." He gave me a dejected look.

"I do."

"Then you should trust me enough to believe I would never take advantage of you...*ever*." He leaned back in his seat. "Shit, you the one with all the power. I'm the one begging."

I blinked and my eyes started leaking.

"I'm crazy about you, Ma." He stared at me with fire in his eyes.

"I've been through so much and done so much. I've got a lot of pain in my heart. But I deal with it every day. With a smile on my face, but internally I'm hurting bad,

Mehkai. I wanna be loved. I do. And I know you would love me so good."

"Then let me love you," he pleaded. "I need to know how you was hurt to make sure I never do that or ever let it happen to you again."

"I'm damaged," I cried, sniffing. "Like...I know I can't be fixed."

"I swear to God, Blaze, my intentions ain't to hurt you, Ma. I'm tryna do the complete opposite."

I sat up, wiping my face.

He continued. "Whatever happened before, I'm sorry. I'll take the blame and work extra hard to build you back up. Let me mend the wounds them other clown niggas caused. You gotta give yourself to me, though."

"Mehkai..."

"You're everything I've ever wanted in a woman, Blaze Santiago." He shook his head. "You special as fuck and you don't even know it, man." He sounded annoyed and looked disappointed.

"I don't know what to say." I'd never had a man be so open about the way he felt about me. Yet here Mehkai was doing just that. They say never judge a book by its cover because you might miss an amazing story. And they were right. Mehkai's pages were astounding. His tough exterior did no justice for how phenomenal his interior was.

"Let me love on you, Blaze. You deserve it. And stop crying." He licked his lips.

"What if you get tired of me? I'm in Kansas City and you're in New York. How will it work? What about Monique?" I babbled on. Long distance relationships rarely ever worked. It didn't help that Mehkai was irresistible.

"I could never get tired of that face, that smile, or that laugh," he assured me. "I'm not asking you to marry me tomorrow." He must've seen the doubt in my eyes. "It's all about *you*. You're the most important piece on my chess board."

My stomach was full of butterflies.

"You can't run from me every time shit gets rough 'cause I'm a street nigga, Ma. My life is hectic. I need to know you in my corner. Shit, I'm damaged too." He laid his head back on the headrest and sighed. He ran his hand across the top of his head and then looked at me.

My heart fluttered. I'd been so wrapped up in my own fears, I never stopped to consider Mehkai was hurting too. Again, we sat silent as I registered everything he'd just said. No relationship was perfect; with joy comes pain.

That's just the way the world worked. Who was I to punish him for the agony I'd endured from my past?

Mehkai had a past too. I remember the first time I looked into his eyes. Pain and strength ran through them. Mehkai was a born survivor. Here he was trying to build me up when he himself was broken. I admired him for that.

"You gon' let me love on you, crybaby?" He broke my train of thought.

I tittered, wiping my face. He gave a one-sided smile. *Lord, those dimples.*

"Only if you let me love on you." My heart answered for me.

"Word?" He leaned forward, staring intently at me.

I smiled. "Word."

"Bet." He started his car. "I'm on my way."

Chapter Six

What are you afraid of?

Kenya

"Blaze, I'm dead ass," I spoke into the phone, eating an Oreo cookie.

"*Dead ass?* Really, Kenya?" She snickered. "You hang with Cole too much."

I laughed. "Don't be hating." She was right, though. I'd been spending a lot of my free time with Cole.

"So Mrs. Campbell..." She giggled. "How's everything with you and the hubby?"

"You're funny." I shook my head. "He had a flight back to New York earlier today. Said Kai needed him for something," I pouted.

"Oh, well, not to be messy or start anything, but *Mehkai* is laying here sleep," she told me, and everything around me stopped.

"What?!"

"Yeah, he's asleep. He's not leaving until Tuesday."

"Blaze, let me call you right back."

She smacked her lips. "Did I get Cole in trouble?"

Hell fuckin' yeah! "No," I stated calmly. "I just want to call and check on him."

"Okay. Meet me for lunch at the Cheesecake Factory around one or one thirty tomorrow."

"Sounds like a date." I quickly hung up with Blaze and immediately called Cole. The phone rang until I was getting ready to hang up.

"What up, gangster?" I could hear the smile in his sexy voice.

"Where are you?"

"Taking care of business. What's wrong? You miss me?"

"No."

"Lie."

"I thought you had to get back to New York to help Kai with something." I waited for him to lie. Cole and I weren't exclusive, but what was understood didn't need to be explained.

"I did."

"How is that when I just got off the phone with Blaze and Kai is over her house sleep?" I shot up off the bed and onto my feet.

"Okay?"

"Okay, Cole you're so full of shit." I began pacing the floor. "What hoe got you running back to New York?"

He chuckled.

"What the hell is so funny?" I didn't find shit comical. "You're a liar, Cole."

"Shut up with all the rah-rah shit, Kenya. Ain't nobody lied to your insecure ass. I told you I had shit to handle. Either take my word or stress yourself out over nothing. Either way, I'm good."

Ugh. I can't stand his arrogant ass.

"I just gave you some act right earlier. What you whining for?"

I'd bet money his signature smirk was in full effect. "You could've stayed." I wasn't ready to let up. "Kai stayed."

"Yo, Kai is Kai, and I'm *Cole*," he snapped. "Is that what you called for? To inform me about what the next nigga got up?"

"No."

"Then what do you want, Kenya? I'm out here tryna make moves. Did you need something?" he asked in a condescending tone.

"You know what? I'ma just stop calling your phone." Cole had a way of getting under my skin like no other.

51

"Now why would you do that? Aye!" he yelled. "Come here, son and let me rap wit' you!" he hollered at somebody in his background. "Where the fuck is my money, nigga?"

I listened on as he spoke to someone letting them know they had six minutes to come back with all the money they owed him and not a penny less.

I cleared my throat. "Why are you so mean, Cole?" I'd be lying if I said his thug mentality didn't wet my panties. However, the lifestyle that came with it was dangerous. Any wrong move or simple mistake could cost him his life.

"Mean?" He chuckled.

t was crazy how he could go from threatening someone's life to laughing and joking with me.

"Yeah...*mean*..."

"I'm not mean, I'm just about my paper. What up, Nas?" he greeted someone else.

"Cole, I'll just call you later when you're not busy."

"I thought you was gon' stop calling my phone altogether." I heard the smile in his voice.

"I was."

"What made you change your mind?"

"I don't know," I answered honestly. "I guess I like your ugly self."

"What you like about me?" he asked, catching me off guard. I didn't expect for him to ask me that. I didn't know he cared.

I sat back down on my bed, pulling a pillow onto my lap. "I like you because since I've met you, you've always been there when it mattered the most." I thought back to our first encounter, shaking my head. "I was pissed about my car and I wanted to go home and cry my eyes out. Not because of my car situation, but because shit in my life had me down. Jamarcus, he ..." I stopped. "Anyway, there you were, a perfect stranger, making me smile and laugh when I didn't want to. That day you came to my house and let me cry in your arms." I squeezed the pillow. "You don't know how much that meant to me, Cole. You cared. You didn't approve of me crying, but you stayed and helped me realize my worth. You made me feel important when I felt like shit."

Squeezing my legs shut, I closed my eyes. "The things you do to my body are indescribable; so indescribable they make me crazy over you to the point that I don't want to share you. I refuse to share you."

I paused. Maybe I'd said too much. Cole had women flocking to him day in and out. What made me any different? I slowly started to regret the decision I'd made to tell him how I felt. *Kenya...really? You know better than that.* "Hello?" His sudden quietness gave me an eerie feeling.

"I'm here."

"Say something." *Say anything, Cole. Damn.* I now felt foolish.

"Yo, Kenya, you ill as fuck."

That's it!? I pulled my phone away from me ear, irritation etched on my face. *I just poured my heart out to your bitch ass and I'm ill as fuck?*

"Thanks," I said dryly, rolling my eyes to the ceiling.

Again...he started talking to the people in his background.

"Cole, I'll talk you later, okay?" I was over our whole conversation and him too.

"Cool. Ayo, take off a couple of days next week and let me know what days you picked."

"For what?"

"Just do it so I can have your plane ticket ready."

"Plane ticket to *where*?"

"I'ma holla at you later. Tell Giggles to quit instigating." He hung up the phone.

Going to Blaze's number in my favorites, I sent a quick text.

Cole

"You straight?" Nasir asked, passing me the blunt.

"Yeah. Why you ask?"

"Nigga, you out here daydreaming." He shook his head, breaking down more weed to roll.

"Nah, I'm just thinking about some stupid shit."

"Must have something to do with shorty you just hung up on." He nodded as if he was seeing right through me. And that shit made me feel uneasy.

When I asked Kenya what she liked about me, I wasn't banking on her response to be so *genuine*. I had bitches reminding me every day how much they *liked* a nigga. But I knew it was because I was paid. For the life of me, I didn't get how they claimed to *like* me when I always fucked and dipped. What was there to like about that?

Taking a long pull from the blunt, I looked down the street. Even though it was cold, the block was hot as fuck. Corner boys were posted, hoes were hanging out on stoops, and shorties were running around playing tag. I adjusted my grey Northface jacket and took another hit before passing it back to Nasir.

The only woman I'd ever loved besides my mother, God rest her soul, was my baby's mother, which meant other than my daughter, Tati, LaRell was the only female I'd ever cared for. Shit with us didn't work out, and I can't front and say I didn't hurt from it, but that was then and this is now. I didn't have time to babysit no bitch.

Nasir passed me the blunt again.

Then there was Kenya. My lil gangster. Somebody who didn't know my paper was long when she met me. She didn't know of my murderous reputation. Didn't know the shit I was capable of, period. I took a toke and then exhaled slowly from my nostrils. Kenya didn't look at me and see dollar signs or power.

I hurriedly shook her from my thoughts. Took another pull from the blunt as I quickly scoped out my surroundings. Fiends were walking around begging for a free fix. Gunshots could be heard a few blocks away. Making sure my burner was secure on my hip, I looked down at my grey Timbs. Passing the blunt to Nasir, I stood up.

"Yo, I'm out," I let him know, descending the raggedy steps slowly.

"A'ight." He nodded, looking down at his phone. "Peace."

"One." I nodded heading towards my brand new Escalade.

"Cole!"

I heard my name being called by a bitch, but I kept on walking.

"Cole, wait!"

I made it to my driver's side as the chick who was calling me made it to my truck.

"Damn, Cole." She giggled. "I know you heard me screaming your name."

I looked down at her trying to remember where I knew shorty from because she looked familiar.

"You don't remember me, do you?" She pouted placing her hands into her coat pocket.

"Should I?" I eyed her as she began to fidget under my gaze.

"I mean I would think you'd remember somebody who sucked you off just a couple weeks ago." She shook her head, looking up at me sadly.

I squinted.

"This shit is so embarrassing, yo." She huffed. "Remember I met you at the corner store and..."

"Ah shit." I bobbed my head. "Yeah, I remember you, shorty. What you doing out here?" I asked, but I didn't care. As soon as the answer left her lips, I would hop in my truck and speed off on her.

"I live over here. I been waiting on your call. But I see you forgot all about me," she said with a lazy grin.

I shrugged.

"Can I take a ride with you?" She licked her lips with hopeful eyes.

"Nah...not today..." I opened my door.

"Um, okay. Well, do you still have my number? Maybe when you're not busy we could hang out," she pressed.

I sighed, hopping into my truck. Removing my gun from my hip, I sat it in my lap and took my phone out of my pocket. "What's your name?"

She frowned. "I told you. Nevermind. It's Remi. I saved it in your phone last time." She looked down the street.

I scrolled through my contacts and her number was indeed saved. "A'ight. I'll hit you up later." I waited for her to step away from the door before I closed it.

Once she was a decent distance away from my truck, I cranked it up and rolled my window down. "Answer the phone."

She nodded and I pulled off.

***

Seven hours later ...

"I can't believe you actually called me." Remi cheesed opening the door wider for me to enter.

"Yeah, I was just passing through. Who here with you?" My eyes skimmed around her small living room.

"Just me and my son." She shut the door.

"He sleep?"

"Yeah, I just put him to bed. You hungry?"

"Nah." I followed her down the short hallway as she led me to her bedroom. On the way, she stopped at a door that had Spider-Man stickers on it. Opening it, she poked her head inside for a second and then shut it back.

"Yep. He's out cold." She smiled.

"A'ight."

We entered her room and I shut the door. Leaning against it, I watched her saunter over to her full size bed.

Remi was thick in all the right places. Nice thick thighs that traveled up to a big ass. She was wearing a sports bra that held perky double D's, boy shorts, and stripped tube socks. I licked my lips at her tattooed body as she slid onto the bed.

This bitch is bad.

I guess I never really took the time to look her over. Remi was what most would consider *thick*. Her stomach wasn't washboard flat, it actually held a little pudge, but that shit was still sexy as fuck. The entire left side of her body, from her shoulder to her juicy leg, was decorated in colorful flowers and butterflies.

Pushing off the door, I slipped my coat off and tossed it to the side. I pulledmy shirt and tank top over my head and tossed them too.

"You know exactly what you came for, huh?" She smirked.

I took the condom out of my back pocket and came out of my jeans and stood over her. Remi was sexy as hell. Her short wavy hair was dark red, bringing out the glow of her caramel skin. She bit down on her full, pouty, bottom lip as she stared at me with those sexy bedroom eyes.

I yanked her panties off roughly and threw them on the floor. Ripping the condom open, I quickly slid it on my dick and leaned over her. She smelled fresh, which was a major bonus. I gripped her hips as she spread her legs open. *Soft as hell.* I slid in inch by inch and she wrapped her arms around my back.

"Damn, Cole, your dick feels so good," she purred in my ear. Her pussy kept pulling me in. I continued to plunge in and out of her wetness as she coated the condom.

"Oh...my...God, Cole," she whimpered scraping her long nails down my back. "I'm 'bout to cum, Daddy!"

Going harder, I rose up so she could get her nails out of my back.

"Fuuuuuck!" She yelled as I pulled out and flipped her over roughly. She immediately arched her back and clapped her ass.

"Damn." I smacked her ass and palmed it as I entered her from behind.

"Shit! Uhn-uhn! Shit!" she cried out, trying to run.

"Nah, yo thick ass gone take this dick, Remi." I slammed her ass hard.

"It...hurts...so good, baby." It sounded like she was crying. She fell forward on her face.

Fuck.

Remi was the bomb.

Chapter Seven

Lovers and friends

Kai

"Damn, Ma, you heavy handed." I joned as Blaze sat on my back giving me a shoulder massage.

She giggled. "Shut up, punk. You're tense."

"That don't mean cave my back in."

"Oh hush." She leaned forward and kissed the back of my neck.

"That shit do feel good, though." I flexed my back.

"Ooouu. That was sexy." She rubbed her oily-ass hands down my back. "Do it again."

I flexed.

"Can you teach me how to do that?"

"Fuck no."

"Why not?" She laughed, still massaging my back.

"Cause flexin' ain't sexy on a woman. Y'all supposed to be cotton candy soft. Not muscular flexin' like you got a dick," I schooled her silly ass.

"Relax. I was just playing." She tittered.

"I know."

"I don't want you to leave." I couldn't see her, but I knew she was pouting.

"Why not?"

"Because I'ma miss you."

That shit made my heart smile. Blaze was being more open with her feelings for me, and it made me feel like a fuckin' king.

"When you were little what did you want to be?" She traced her nails across my tattoos.

"A gangster."

She smacked her lips.

"What?"

"When you were a little boy in elementary and your friends were talking about being doctors, firefighters, and lawyers, you wanted to be a *gangster*?" she asked like she didn't believe me.

"Yeah."

"Why? That's stupid." She sighed, pushing down on my shoulders hard.

I flipped her over gently and she landed on her side facing me. *Fuckin' beautiful.* Even with her eyebrows drawn down into a frown. Her dark brown eyes stared deep into mine, and for a second I got lost in our gaze.

What the fuck is she doin' to me.

I looked away tracing her body with my hand.

"How I grew up, Blaze...That's why."

She shifted, scooting closer to me. "Tell me about it?" Even though it should've been a statement, it came out like a question. I respected that.

"Where you want me to start?" Our eyes connected again.

"From the beginning." She broke eye contact to snuggle closer to me. With her small body tucked underneath mine, she waited.

I contemplated on giving Blaze the clean version of my past. Afraid that the gruesome shit I've seen and done throughout my life might turn her off and she'd run from me again. A part of me, the savage in me, didn't know if I could fully trust Blaze with secrets from my life. Nobody...not even Camille could get me to open up about myself. Some things were better left unsaid.

I must've taken too long to answer because Blaze cleared her throat and rubbed my back lightly. "Tell me about your mom." Her soft voice relaxed me. I hadn't even realized I'd tensed up, unintentionally putting my guard up.

"What that nigga, Pac, say? She's my heart in human form...my best friend."

"I can tell." She wrapped her left arm around me.

"Yea, she strong. Been through a lot with me, my pops, and her family. Ma Duke is a soldier."

"How did she feel about you wanting to be a gangster?"

"She wasn't feeling it, but she understood. My father left us when I was going on maybe three years old. Moms was maybe nineteen at the time. I don't remember much, but I remember her crying *a lot*. Anyway, as I grew up, we were staying in these projects off Twelfth Street. I was hanging with jack boys and drug dealers at a young age...like nine or ten."

"Mmm..." She sighed.

"By the time I was thirteen, I was hitting licks and stealing cars. Every time I got in trouble my mother would try to keep me locked in the house and shit. Beat my ass then ground me." I chuckled, thinking back on how lethal my mother's hands used to be.

"Her punishments wouldn't last long, though. As soon as she had to leave for work, I was right back hugging the block."

Blaze shook her head. "Bad ass."

"I caught my first case when I was fourteen. Joy riding, high and drunk, in a stolen whip. They searched the car, found weed and the gun my dumb ass had tucked underneath my seat. I ended up in juvie. Broke my mother's heart. She wouldn't even come see me."

I looked over and down at Blaze. "Fast forward a couple years, I'm gang affiliated, moving dope for one of the biggest crime families out of Florida. Ended up moving down there, following this little chick I was fuckin' with.

"How long did you stay in Florida?"

"For a couple months. Camille was the first shorty I'd ever invested time in. Well... wasted time on." I paused. "So to answer your first question, I didn't want to be a doctor, a lawyer nor firefighter because that's not what I was accustomed to. They weren't my heroes. They weren't the ones who took me in, showed me love, how to be a man, get money and make shit happen. *Gangsters* did. And they were all I knew so I wanted to be like them. Nice clothes, cars, bitches and mad money. That was my goal. Even if it meant disappointing my mother."

"And the teardrops?" Her index finger traced the tattoos on my face.

66

"I've done my dirt."

Blaze

Even with Mehkai telling me about his ugly past, he was still beautiful to me. I could sense he was giving me the PG version, but I understood. For him to even consider me a confidant made me feel important. Worthy for someone like him.

"Tell me about your mother." He turned on his side to face me. "Where she at?"

I slowly pulled away from him. It felt like the room was closing in on me. All from a simple question. *Where is she?* I didn't know and I didn't care, but I did at the same time. Because even though I despised my mother, I loved her to death. Even in her absence, she played a major role in my life. Despondency.

"She's somewhere living her life." I shrugged, attempting to get out of the bed. Mehkai quickly, but gently pulled me back close to him.

"What I say about running?" I closed my eye as the beat of his heart put me back at ease. "I got you," he said in a low tone.

And again, I believed him. Not only because of the sincerity in his voice, but because I could feel it. In his chest and in mine too. Our two heartbeats became one steady one.

"She got remarried. Started a family with my dad's best...well *ex-best* friend. I was twelve when she left. I loved her. I thought she loved me too."

"I'm sure she does." Mehkai tried to convince me.

"Apparently, not as much as she loves her other kids. They have her. They know her. The real her." If my mother did love me, she had a horrible way of showing it.

The room became silent as a huge part of me wanted to pull away from the conversation. Yeah, Mehkai's father had left him, but he could barely walk or talk when it happened. That didn't make it any better, but I was twelve...almost a teenager. I had built a friendship, love, respect, and trust, for a person who decided one day she'd rather be with a black man. Years of foundation were broken. Mehkai didn't know his father, but just like him, my mother was once my best friend.

"You're a smart woman, Blaze. You're beautiful too."
He caressed my cheek. "I swear to God you one in a million."
He cupped my chin. "Your moms missed out on the dope
person you've grown to be. And you did that shit without
her, Ma."

I could feel tears burning my eyes. Why did he have
to look at me like that? Like...how I felt and what I was going
through mattered to him. Like all my problems were
officially his too.

Damn it, Mehkai. I looked away as I attempted to
blink my tears away. "Thank you."

"You know we could share my mother." He shrugged.
"She's cool for the most part. Nosy as hell, but slim means
well."

I couldn't help but laugh as he pulled me closer.

"You got me feeling slippery as fuck," he grumbled.

"I had to sop your sexy ass up." I giggled.

He shook his head. "Now, I'ma damn biscuit. Ain't
that some shit?" He rose up. "Take your shirt off," he
demanded.

Sliding my shirt over my head, I exposed my naked
body. Leaving me in only my fluffy cheetah print socks.

"Mmm..." Mehkai groaned, grabbing his dick through his briefs, which made me blush. "Hand me that bacon grease." He nodded towards the coconut oil I was just rubbing him down with.

I tittered, handing it over. "You're so silly." And I loved it.

Sitting on the edge of my bed, he pulled my feet onto his lap. After removing my socks, he sat them next to him. I watched in lust as he skillfully poured the warm oil over and between my toes. Gently massaging my toes with his left hand, his right thumb massaged the bottom of my foot.

"You're beautiful as fuck, Ma," he told me for the twentieth time since we woke up. But I didn't mind. I loved hearing it, especially from him. His opinion meant everything to me.

"Thank you, baby," I cooed, truly grateful.

We sat in comfortable silence as he tenderly caressed my feet and toes. I kept stealing glances at the perfect specimen in front of me. The plethora of tattoos on his body were big and bold. Those lips that I used to dream about kissing looked better than ever. Maybe because they were all mine.

When he finished with my feet, he poured the oil along my thighs.

"Mmm..." I moaned as his big hands squeezed on my upper thighs. "That feels good."

My phone ringing brought me down from my natural high. Looking at the silver clock on my nightstand, I saw it was damn near midnight. *Must be Kenya.*

I reached for my phone and rolled my eyes. Mason.

Mehkai now had my legs spread and was positioned between them, rubbing the oil on my inner thighs and stomach. My phone continued ringing.

"Who is that?"

I could've lied and said it was Kenya or ignored his call and continued to get my rub down. But I quickly remembered how Mehkai felt about me lying to him. "Mason."

He smirked and nodded. "Answer."

"What? Why?" I was in a good mood. Mason would ruin it.

"'Cause I said so."

I sighed. But like an obedient child, I pressed the green icon and put it on speaker.

"What, Mason?" I smacked my lips. Mehkai kissed my stomach.

"Why are you ignoring me?"

Mehkai's soft lips slid down my freshly shaven kitty. He planted a juicy kiss right on my clit that made me forget all about answering Mason. Biting the inside of my right thigh he sent a chill from the tip of my toes to the top of my head. I closed my eyes as he blew on my clit. When his wet tongue flicked across my swollen pearl, I almost lost it.

"Blaze!" Mason called my name.

"Ssshit..." Kai hungrily took me into his mouth, slurping, sucking, and nibbling. "Baby..." I arched my back as he laid on his stomach, wrapping his arms around my thighs.

I looked down to see the work my baby was putting in, and our eyes connected.

"Ooooh, baby! Yes, right there, baby, don't stop," I begged loudly.

"Are you fuckin' serious!" Mason bellowed through the receiver.

"Mmm..." Kai moaned into my sex.

"Baby, I'm cumming." I rocked my hips. "Ooh, I'm cumming, daddy!" My clit felt like it was about to explode.

I don't know when I dropped my phone, but I held onto the back of Mehkai's head as I humped his face roughly.

"Yeeesss!" I screamed out, body jerking and toes pointed. "Fuck!"

Mehkai kissed me softly up my stomach, licked my pierced nipples, and sucked on the front of my neck. I shivered from his touch.

"Whose pussy is this, Blaze?" he asked into my ear. Before I could answer, he was filling me up, causing my voice to get stuck in my throat. How did he expect me to form a sentence, hell a *word*, feeling this good? How could he not know what he was doing to me? He licked on my earlobe, winding his hips, slamming inside of me.

"Baby..." was all I could manage in a weak whisper. It would have to do.

"Whose pussy is this, Blaze?" he asked again, still winding his hips.

My eyes rolled to the back of my head and I silently thanked God for putting Kai in my life. I wrapped my arms around his back and he went deeper.

"It's yours, baby! Kaaiii!"

73

He kissed my lips. "Yo pussy wet as fuck, Ma. Open your eyes, baby." He planted another wet kiss on my lips as I did what I was told.

"This yo' dick, Blaze," he assured me, biting down on my bottom lip.

"Oh my God!" I yelled out as I felt my orgasm building. Soon after, I released on his dick and all over my sheets.

Mehkai laid his body on top of mine. Biting down on my collar, he mumbled a few words I couldn't make out. His body then rested on mine. All that could be heard in the room was our heavy, labored breathing. That was until I heard a shuffling sound coming from my phone.

"Blaze!"

Is this fool still on my phone? I couldn't believe Mason would sit on the phone and listen to me have sex. Kai grabbed my phone and brought it close to our faces.

"Don't call this number again." The soft look in his eyes had been replaced with hard menacing ones. The same ones I'd seen him give me the night I didn't listen at the strip club.

Mason was about to say something, but Kai hung up on him. Rolling off of me, he laid on his back. "Get on top."

He pulled me by my arm. "Show Daddy how much you gon'miss me."

Chapter Eight

New Jack City

Kai

I watched as everybody filed in and started taking their seats around the wide table. It was going on four in the morning, but I was wide awake. I had business to conduct. My cousin, Jamarcus, walked in talking on the phone, and like I knew he would, Cole glanced in my direction. Cocking my head to the side, I waited for him to take his seat.

Once I was sure everyone was in attendance, I cleared my throat and all eyes were on me. "What up? I'm glad you niggas could finally make it." I smirked and they all started chuckling. Jamarcus was still on his phone.

I slowly made my way to where he was seated. "As you know, we got some beef out in Philly. Niggas out there been mad disrespectful." Rubbing my hands together, I kept my eyes on Jamarcus, who was *still* on his phone. Here I was speaking on disrespect, and my own flesh and blood was dead-ass doing just that.

"Niggas know how I feel about disrespect right?" Everybody's eyes were on me as I pulled my gun from my waist. Coming up behind Jamarcus, I took the butt of my gun and slammed down hard on the top of his dome.

His head hit the table first and then his body hit the floor with a loud thud. "Everybody get the fuck out!" I yelled now infuriated. Jamarcus was family and all, but we weren't close enough to be pulling no shit like this.

I could hear the hustle of everybody as they rushed out. Cole, Nas, and Quan stayed. Jamarcus attempted to get up. "What...what the fuck man?" He held the top of his head.

Yanking him up by his shirt collar, I shoved him back into his seat. "Yo, why the fuck you got that fuckin' phone in here!" My fist came down hard, crashing into his nose.

"Aye, Kai, man, come on," he begged, shielding his face.

Cole laughed.

I didn't find shit funny. I didn't have room for any kind of slips ups. Everybody knew not to bring a fuckin' phone in this room. When Jamarcus begged me to put him on, I told him he would get the same treatment as every man on my team. There wasn't no family leisure. He held on to his nose, mugging me.

"Yo, this nigga 'bout to cry." Cole laughed. "Pussy-ass nigga, son."

Nasir snickered.

Snatching his phone from the table, I tossed it to Quan, who caught it and left the room.

"Kai, I'm family. You really doing this?" His mug deepened. "That's fucked up," he spat, still holding onto his nose.

"Yeah, this nigga finna cry." Cole sat down on the table. "I don't know what the fuck Kenya saw in his bitch ass."

At the mention of Kenya's name, Jamarcus jumped up. "The fuck you just say?" He started for Cole.

Cole stood up. "Nigga, you heard me." He swiftly removed the gun from behind his back and pointed it to Jamarcus' head as he approached him. He stopped walking almost immediately. Cole smirked. "Nah, bring yo' tough ass over here. I been itchin' to murk a nigga."

Jamarcus shook his head and then looked over in my direction. "Kai, you gon' let this nigga pull a gun out on yo' family?" He looked to me for help.

"That petty shit y'all trippin' on ain't got shit to do with me. Bring another phone in here and I'ma show you just what family out here mean." I didn't wanna have to kill my cousin 'cause I knew my mother's twin sister would probably die right next to him of a broken heart. But if I had to, I would and then pay for the entire funeral service.

"A'ight..." Jamarcus nodded his head. "You gon' definitely get yours." His eyes shifted back to Cole.

"I doubt that." Cole seemed unbothered as he sat back down at the table with his gun sitting next to him.

"When you talk to Kenya tell her *thank you* for me. I was just over there dropping my seeds off in her." He grabbed his nuts. "Released a well-needed nut." He smirked.

Before Nasir could grab him, Cole picked his gun up and shot Jamarcus in his leg. Hopping up from the table, he walked toward Jamarcus pointing his gun at him.

"Aaaagghhh!"Jamarcus cried out. Holding onto his leg, he rocked back and forth. "Fuuuuuccck." He looked over at me, pleading with his eyes for me to step in. I smirked at him instead.

"I told you this nigga was 'bout to cry." Nasir sneered, now leaning over him. "Open yo' mouth, pussy." He grabbed Jamarcus roughly by the front of his shirt and hit him in the face with his burner. "Open yo' fuckin' mouth!" He yelled this time.

Jamarcus slowly did what he was told and Cole stuffed the burner in his mouth. "Who the fuck you think you talkin' to, nigga." I watched as Cole's eyes turned black. He was in murder-man mode.

Jamarcus cried his response as snot and tears ran down his distressed face.

"Nah, talk that hot shit now, b." Cole glared down at him. "You mad cause Kenya fuckin' wit a real nigga now, huh?" he asked rhetorically. If my cousin had any sense, he knew not to say a word.

"Kai, Nas, this nigga mad 'cause I took his bitch." His eyebrows drew down further. "Yeah..." his voice trailed off as he nodded his head. "I should kill yo' punk ass for disrespectin'."

Jamarcus' eyes widened in fear.

"Apologize, nigga." Cole put his finger on the trigger.

"I'm...I'm sorry," Jamarcus cried, with gun still in his mouth and tears falling like rain.

"For what?" Cole smiled, eyes still black.

"For disrespecting you?" The blood from his leg started soaking up the carpet.

"And for what else?" Cole asked.

Jamarcus gave him a confused look. "I..."

"Say you sorry for being a bitch nigga," Cole demanded.

Nasir laughed.

Jamarcus shook his head before looking over at me. I stared right back. Him being stupid is what got him here. Couldn't even follow simple directions. All of this could've been avoided had he not brought a fuckin' phone in here. I was still pissed.

Jamarcus faced Cole again when he saw I wasn't gon' save him. "I'm...sorry for being..." He gave a defeated sigh. "I'm...I'm sorry for being a...a...a bitch nigga." He blinked and the tears started again.

"Where you find this simp-ass nigga, Kai Money?" Nasir sat down in a vacant seat. "Nigga ain't even willing to die for self-respect." He shook his head in disappointment.

Cole removed his burner from Jamarcus' mouth and wiped it on his shirt. "Spitting and shit."

"Kai," Jamarcus cried real-life tears. "I need to go to the hospital, I'ma bleed to the death." He pressed down on his leg. "Get me to a doctor, man," he begged.

"Walk yo' stupid ass to the hospital then." I started walking toward the door.

"What?" he asked and I stopped to face him. "I'll die, man. I'm family, Kai. Our mamas are twins, bro. Blood is thicker than water," he rambled off.

"You right." I nodded my head in Cole's direction. "Kill him."

Cole swiftly placed his gun on Jamarcus' forehead. "Wait!" he yelled. "Wait…" He hung his head. "I'll walk to the hospital."

"You sure?" I asked, eyeing him.

"Yeah…yeah, man. I'll walk."

I shrugged. "A'ight." Cole sucked his teeth as we exited the room with Nasir following close behind. "Yo, Nas, turn that light off. Electric bill was high as fuck this month." He turned back around to the cut the light off in the room.

Cole and I made it outside and into the building's parking lot no more than five minutes later. "You shoulda let me body his ass." He started toward his truck.

"Nah, let that nigga live until I say otherwise." Jamarcus bringing his phone into an important meeting still had me hot. Why the fuck would he even try me like that? Did he not believe me when I said I would kill him if I had to? Why the fuck did he think he would get a pass? A single rain drop landed on my nose, jolting me from my thoughts.

"A'ight." He nodded, opening the driver's door just as Nasir was coming out of the building's double glass doors.

"That nigga in there crying like a baby." He laughed, walking toward his bike.

"Nigga, it's 'bout to rain and yo' ass hopping on a bike?" Cole hopped in and shut the door. Starting the truck, he rolled his windows down. "Only nigga I know riding motorcycles in the dead of winter and shit." He snickered. Nasir put his middle finger up as Cole pulled off.

"What you getting into, Kai Money?" he asked, hopping on his bike.

"Shit, I don't know. Turn a couple corners, slide down a few blocks." I opened the driver's door to my G-wagon.

"Straight." He placed a red racer helmet on top of his head. "Yo, it's gon' be a long night for ya boy." He nodded toward the building.

The rain picked up. "Yeah, I know." I looked up at the dark building. There were no phones inside and all the lights were cut off. The cleanup crew wouldn't be coming until the afternoon. And from the way blood seemed to running out of his leg, he needed to get to a doctor. He'd rode with the lil homey, Rylo, so technically, he was stranded. He'd have to crawl in the freezing rain to the hospital, which was a thirty minute car ride away.

"He gon' be a problem." Nas pulled his helmet down over her face. Revving his bike up a few times, he shot me a head nod and peeled off.

Closing my car door, I started the car and looked up at the building again. What Nas said resonated. Jamarcus didn't have the balls to beef with me so that was the least of my concerns. The only thing that worried me was how much he already knew about my operation. He didn't come off as no rat, but an embarrassed man was probably worse than a scorned woman. If Jamarcus made it through the night, me and him were going to have a long conversation.

Chapter Nine

Baby mama...not wifey

Cole

After the meeting that was supposed to have been a priority, I found myself heading toward Trenton. The hour drive gave me an ample amount of time to think about my next move with Kenya. I ain't gon' lie. Hearing Jamarcus say he'd seen her recently, when she wasn't answering my calls was fuckin' with me. What the fuck was he doing anywhere near her? If she had let him fuck her, I was gon' kill him and strangle her ass.

The hour drive to Trenton seemed to have been shortened as I pulled into LaRell's driveway. Looking at my dashboard, I saw it was going on six-thirty in the morning. *What the fuck you doin' here, son?* I ran my left hand down my face and turned the ignition off. Tati didn't have to be up for school until nine.

Exiting my truck, I shut the door and hit the key fob. Taking the stairs two at a time, I reached the door and started banging on it. Pulling my phone out, I pulled LaRell's number up and put the phone to my ear. After a couple rings, she answered.

"What, Cole?" She'd been sleep.

"Come open the door."

She smacked her lips and then I heard tussling on her end. "What do you want, Cole?" She huffed and two minutes later, the locks on her front door clicked. She swung the door open, phone still to her ear, in nothing but lace panties.

Her nipples were hard and the gold nipple hoop in her right nipple glistened. Her hair was pulled up into a messy ponytail. I could never front and say LaRell wasn't one of the sexiest women I'd ever fucked with. Her smooth toffee colored skin was covered in a whole bunch of colorful tattoos and her pretty cat-like eyes were the same color as cognac sitting underneath very thick, long eyelashes. And she was built like a fuckin' brick house.

I pushed past her as she tried to act like she was mad. "Shut the door and come on." I tossed over my shoulder, taking her steps. She closed the door following me close behind.

"Cole, why are you here?" She said with an attitude and shut her bedroom door. "Tati is sleep."

I took my coat off. "Yeah, I know." Sitting on her bed, I reached down to take my Timbs off.

"Why do you keep doing this, Cole?" She stood by the door.

"Yo, LaRell..." I shook my head. "I'm not in the mood for no shit," I informed her dramatic ass.

"So I'm just supposed to be okay with being your doormat, Cole?"

"Man..." She had me second guessing my decision to come over.

"How do you think you jumping in and out of my bed makes me feel, Cole?" She inched toward me.

"I don't care."

"How could you say that?" Her pace picked up. "I'm the mother of your child. We're supposed to be a family. And you don't care about my feelings?" she snapped.

"We *are* family. What the fuck are you talkin' about?" I pulled my shirt over my head, tossing my locs back.

"Then treat me like I'm family. Damn! One minute you on some fuck shit, only dealing with me when it comes to our daughter. But then there are times like now, when you show up on my door step and wanna lay in my bed," she popped off. "I mean what the fuck is up? I'm tired of playing with you."

I waved her off again.

"I'm serious. It's either all or nothing, Cole." She crossed her arms over her chest. "You say we a family, let's be one."

"Yo, LaRell, you already know what's up." I stepped out of my jeans.

"No, I don't."

"Yes, the fuck you do." I glared at her.

"Wooow...." she sung. "I fuck around one time to your how many? Shit, I lost track of count after nine." She got all hostile and shit. Little ass didn't put fear in nobody but Tati.

"That's all it takes," I said coolly, lying down on my back. "You see how that turned out." I said, referring to her son, Mason.

"Then I should've been done," she snapped.

"That's on you." I closed my eyes.

"You still love me, Cole." She sat down on the bed next to me. "I know you do. Your ego is just bigger than your brain."

"Yeah, a'ight."

"No, fuck that. Talk to me. I'm not one of them bitches you fuck and duck. I'm the mother of your fuckin' child, nigga." She swatted me on the arm. "Cole."

"What you want me to say, Rell? I was rockin' wit' you. You the one that stepped out and had a fuckin' baby."

"*After* you did so many different time and got caught. I was hurting, Cole. You had bitches laughing at me, smiling in my face, and fucking you." She shook her head. "You niggas are so backwards. You can get caught fuckin' around twenty different times and a bitch is supposed to automatically forgive you 'cause she loves you. But as soon as you get a little taste of payback, it's the end of the fuckin' world. Stop it."

"You ain't love me."

"Really? You can fix your mouth to say that shit to me? After all we've been through. After all I've sacrificed for us? You actually believe that bullshit?"

"What's done is done, Rell. Lay down and go to sleep."

"So that's it? You don't want this no more? You don't want your family?" She scoffed in disbelief.

I closed my eyes, ignoring her

"I know you love me, Cole. That's why even though I hurt you, you can't leave me alone. We go without talking for too long, and you come looking for me. Even when I just tried to be on that co-parenting tip, you was damn near begging to get back in my bed. I had a baby, but you hurt me too, Cole."

"You want me to go sleep in the guest room?" I asked, getting ready to sit up.

"See. And what about Tatiana? She loves waking up with you here. You don't think we're giving her the wrong impression?"

"Do yo' other baby daddy gotta hear this bullshit all night?" I knew I would hit a nerve with that. I understood Rell was used to how we used to be, but shit was different now. We weren't sixteen no more, and after she had Mason, I couldn't even look at her the same. What really fucked me up was she had fucked a nigga who didn't give two fucks about her or Mason. "Do you want me to go sleep in another room?"

The room became silent. I had to open one eye to make sure she was still there. She stared back at me with a hurt look plastered on her pretty face. *If she 'bout to start that crying shit, I'm leaving and going back to New York.*

"Fine," she huffed, standing up. "I'm done trying, Cole. I'ma start dating." She climbed into the bed next to me.

"Yeah...a'ight."

"I'm serious. So don't be mad when change comes." She turned her back to me dramatically.

Blaze

"Hey, Blaze!" I heard Cassandra before I seen her.

I stopped in my tracks to face her. She walked toward me with who I knew to be her twin sister, Camille. I'd never met her before, but she and Cassandra were identical. The only difference was their hair. Cassandra's was shoulder length, and Camille was sporting a pixie cut.

"Hey, Cassandra." I smiled as they approached me.

"What's up, girl." She playfully hit my arm. "This is my sister, Camille. Camy, remember you asked me who did the painting in my living room. Well, here she is?" She grinned.

I held my hand out. "Nice to finally meet you."

She took it. "Girl, you talented as hell." She smiled. "I told Cassy to ask you if you could hook me up with something."

"Of course." I pulled my phone out of my coat pocket. "Here put your number in here." Handing it to her, I watched as she keyed her number in and called herself from my phone.

"What you 'bout to do, Blaze?" Cassandra asked as her sister passed me back my phone.

"Go upstairs and chill." Kenya wasn't feeling well, so I was leaving her alone to get some rest. "Maybe read a book or something." I had two books on my Kindle that had been in my library for two weeks that I hadn't read yet.

"You should come hang out with us." Camille offered.

"I don't know-"

"Come on Blaze." Cassandra cut in. Let's go to the bar and have drinks. Let me tell y'all about my fucked up love life." She pouted pulling me by my arm.

Camille smiled. "Right, it's Friday. Come kick it with us."

I quickly contemplated on hopping in my bed, or hanging out with the twins. Cassandra was cool and all, but she wasn't the type of chick I'd just hang around. Then I remembered Kenya laughing telling me Cassandra would only keep asking until I did. "Okay." I nodded. If I went this one time, I wouldn't feel bad for every time in the future I told her no. "I'm down." Cassandra linked her arm into mine and led the way towards her Nissan.

***

"So, Blaze, you're a photographer?" Camille scooted her shot glass closer to her.

"Yep." I sipped on my strawberry daiquiri.

"For like magazines and stuff, right?" She took the shots.

"Yeah." I nodded.

"That's dope. Cassandra said you even went to New York recently." She looked over at her sister.

90

"Yeah. I had a shoot for Vogue."

"That's what's up." She eyed me awkwardly.

"So." Cassandra broke the awkward tension. "It's this dude that I'm really feeling." She cheesed back and forth between me and Camille.

"Since when?" Camille seemed uninterested in the conversation. Suddenly her mood was off putting. She seemed annoyed.

"Since about a couple weeks ago." The bartender slid our margaritas towards us.

"Aw." Camille said dryly, pulling another shot towards her.

I cut my eyes at her. "That's good, Cassandra." I smiled. "How'd you meet him?"

"Through a mutual friend." She took a sip. "I'm about to cut his ass off, though. He plays too many games."

"That's all they do," Camille added her two cents.

Mehkai immediately crossed my mind. "Not all men." I placed my glass to my lips. "There are actually good men out there," I informed her. I had one to vouch for. That familiar feeling of butterflies filled my stomach.

She scoffed. "Girl, please. No there ain't. I was with a nigga for years, and I mean *years*, and he acts as if I never existed." She sounded hurt.

I didn't mean to come off nosey, but I wanted to know. "What happened?"

91

"He went to jail. I got pregnant and he stopped fucking with me."

"Wow. I'm sorry."

"Camy, tell the whole truth." Cassandra laughed. "You got pregnant by his cousin and was too scared to keep the baby." She downed the rest of her drink.

"Damn, Cassandra, tell the whole city, why don't you?"

"What? I'm just saying."

"Whatever. Anyways, yes, I slept with his cousin, but it's a good chance the baby could've been his. We were fucking a lot before he got locked up." She glared at Cassandra.

"Then why you didn't keep the baby?" No response. "Exactly. You weren't sure."

"He didn't know, though."

"So why'd he break up with you?" I questioned.

"Because I got the abortion and he thought it was his." She sighed into her glass. "Shit, what was I supposed to do? Raise a baby by myself? Hell no."

"God does everything for a reason," I offered. "Maybe he wanted you to be with someone better. You said he went to jail, and I'm guessing he went for quite a while. God was looking out for you. Nobody needs the extra stress of dealing with a man like that." I tried to make her feel better.

Cassandra snickered, shaking her head. "Maybe you're right, Blaze." She and Cassandra shared a look I'm sure they didn't think I'd noticed.

Camille thought she was sly but I saw when she cut her eyes at me. "Yeah, maybe."

Feeling the tension building again, I gulped the rest of my drink down. "Look, I just remembered I had some work to finish at home." I slid out of my stool, picking my coat up.

"Oh...okay." Cassandra looked over at me. "Camille you ready?" She hopped out of her seat.

"No. I'll take an Uber home." She faced the bar.

"Okaaaay...let's go, Blaze." Cassandra slid her arms into her coat starting towards the door.

"It was nice meeting you, Camille." I smiled.

She didn't even look at me. "Nice meeting you too, Blaze."

Chapter Ten

Hurt people ... *hurt* people

Kenya

"So tell me again why I have to hang out with a group of females I don't know?" I asked Cole with an attitude.

"'Cause I got some quick business to handle, Ma. Quit questioning me and put your fuckin' shoes on." He adjusted the chains around his neck, eyeing me.

"You're an asshole."

He shot me a platinum smile and a quick wink. "Keep on with that slick-ass mouth. I'ma bend your fine ass over this couch again," he threatened.

"Whatever." I reached for the black, red bottoms he'd gifted me upon my arrival.

"That's what I thought."

***

That's how I ended up sitting at a bar with three women I didn't know. I sighed before taking another sip of my Patrón margarita. I nodded a kudos to the bartender for making it extra strong. One of the chicks named Skyy was throwing Patrón shots back like it was water. She was actually a really cool chick although she a stranger. She said she was from Kansas City too and we clicked almost immediately.

Skyy was gorgeous with slanted eyes and high cheek bones. Her long weave had to be at least twenty-four inches long and it was parted down the middle bone straight. The only makeup she wore was gold eye shadow and burgundy matte lipstick. Her skin was a pretty dark chocolate. Skyy reminded me of a little China doll. She pulled another shot toward her, shifting in her seat.

"Let's...let's make a toast" she slurred, raising her shot glass above her head.

"To what?" The chick named Myeisha smacked her shiny lips. "Ain't shit to celebrate, yo," she spat in a thick New York accent.

Myeisha had been acting like that since I met her an hour and a half ago. If she'd stop frowning, she might actually be prettier. Don't get me wrong. Myeisha was cute, but the fucked up attitude took away from her beauty. One side of her head was shaved into a low fade while the other held long, loose curls that dangled close to her face. She was draped in diamonds with one of those "boss bitch" personas. Her long natural lashes flapped as she rolled her eyes.

"Are you mad?" Skyy looked over at her.

"I know y'all ain't 'bout to start." That was Ryan. She was almost as bright as me. The only difference in our skin tones was hers was covered in black ink. Her pink hair was pulled back into a long, sleek ponytail, showcasing her flawlessly made-up face. The small beauty mark above her lip added to her overall uniqueness. Beautiful, but completely down to earth.

Myeisha waved her off. "I swear I'ma curse Nasir the fuck out," she fumed.

"Anyways ..." Skyy rolled her eyes, raising her glass again. "Let's toast."

We each lifted our glasses, with the exception of Myeisha.

"What are we toasting to?" Ryan held up two shots of pineapple Ciroc.

"Life!" Skyy hollered before tossing her drink back.

Ryan and I quickly clinked our glasses together. "To life," we said in unison.

"We celebrating?" I felt Cole wrap his strong arms around me and then kiss the back of my neck.

"Yep...life." I smiled at his embrace.

"Where's Nasir?" Myeisha frowned.

Cole shrugged. "You ready?" He spun the barstool I was on around to face him.

"Where are we going?"

"Back to the room. I got a surprise for you," he whispered in my ear. The feeling of his soft lips had my panties moist. He helped me off the stool, taking my small hand into his large one.

"You look sexy." He pulled me close to him as we made our exit out of the hotel's bar and lounge.

The entire elevator ride to the fifteenth floor, Cole whispered sweet nothings in my ear. He had me gushing, giggling, and just being flat-out girly. And I didn't mind. I couldn't remember feeling like this in so long. He made me feel wanted. Appreciated.

By the time we made it to our floor, our bodies were officially one. He kissed on my neck and chin, reminding how good I looked and smelled. A little thrown off by his sudden display of affection, I pulled away shyly. He walked behind me closely as we made it to the suite, still telling me how fine I was. My cheeks were burning from his compliments.

Once we were inside the room, Cole swiftly picked me up. He carried me to the nearest dresser and sat me on top of it. Standing between my legs, he roughly hiked up my dress and snatched my lace thong down and one quick motion.

"You missed me, huh?" I kissed his chocolate neck.

"Shut up." He smirked, unbuckling his belt, pulling his jeans down.

Reaching down, I pulled his manhood out the top of his briefs. Guiding him into my center, our sexes connected, making my eyes roll to the back of my head.

"Ooooh, baby," I moaned into his ear.

"Fuck, Ma. This pussy tight as fuck." He pulled me closer and plunged deeper into me.

"Cole ..." I wrapped my hands around his neck. "Fuck this pussy, baby," I egged him on, matching his strokes. "Just like that, baby."

He picked me up. Slamming me down on his dick, he stuck his tongue in my mouth, giving me a sloppy kiss. I held onto him as I felt my orgasm rising. *Dick ain't supposed to be this good.*

I bit down on my bottom lip as I came. Cole had me whimpering like a wounded animal.

"FUUUUUCK!" He groaned, biting down on my neck.

"Baby, ouch," I whined.

"Shut up," he mumbled. Breathing hard.

"You shut up." I rolled my eyes as he put me down.

Chuckling, he pulled his Versace shirt over his head. When he did, his shirt knocked the 'man bun' I'd done for him earlier that day over, causing his long locs to cascade down his broad shoulders and back.

"Go run us some shower water." He walked off toward the suite's massive living room area.

"Ask nicely." I stepped out of my dress.

"Just do what I said," he spoke over his shoulder as I slipped my stilettos off.

"Rude ass."

***

Thirty minutes later, we were finally getting out of the shower. Dead tired from all the sexing we'd been doing since we'd gotten to Miami yesterday, I laid across the plush bed on my stomach. The sound of a phone going off made me lay on my side. Cole's phone lit up, letting me know he had an incoming text message. Sitting up on my elbows, I smacked my lips.

"Cole, one of your bitches is blowing your phone up!" I called out to him.

"Word?" He rounded the corner, puffing on a blunt.

Snatching his phone up, I tried reading the notification on the screen. *Remi.*

"Who's Remi?" I asked as he snatched his phone out of my hand.

"Nobody."

"Cole—"

"Yo, Kenya, don't start that insecure shit tonight." Sitting down on the floor in front of the bed, he pushed his locs out of his face. "Come braid my shit back."

Rolling my eyes to the ceiling, I slowly made my way over to where he was sitting. "How many braids do you want?" I asked, trying to look over his shoulder. What the fuck did Remi want? It was going on two in the morning.

"Two." He took another toke.

With him sitting in between my legs, I pulled one side of his hair up and wrapped the rest in a bun. His phone went off again and he placed it next to him. When he leaned forward for the remote to the PlayStation 4 he'd demanded the hotel have ready for him, I saw them. The scratches on his back.

What the hell?!

Instantly I became sick to my stomach. The scratches weren't fresh, but they weren't that old neither. And they weren't mine. My body started overheating as my chest tightened. Why?

Why did I continue to allow these no-good niggas to hurt me? Use me. Lie to me. Make a fool out of me?

Cole leaned back onto the bed, turning the television on.

"I'm 'bout to murder these niggas," he said, letting the blunt hang from the corner of his lips. "Baby, who you want me to play with? Golden State or the Nets?"

The room became silent as the game loaded and he picked through teams. When I didn't respond, he turned slightly to face me. Frowning, he took the blunt out of his mouth and put the controller down.

"What you crying for?"

Cole

I remember when I was a young cat, my uncle would always cater to my aunt. Whatever she wanted, she got. House, cars, shoes, clothes...you name it. I grew up knowing he loved her, but didn't understand why he would go out of his way when he didn't have it, and she didn't deserve it. It was just to appease her. It got so bad, when my aunt didn't get her way, she'd walk around the house miserable and shit.

One day I asked him, though.

"Unc, why you always going out of your way when you can barely afford it. She don't appreciate it anyway."

He smirked. Passed me the blunt we were sharing and looked off into space. "Because your auntie is my queen. And I'd do everything in my power to keep a smile on her face. When she's not happy, I'm not either."

Growing up I never cared about a bitch that much to consider her feelings. I mean my baby's mother was a down-ass chick when we were together. We'd fuss and fight every once in a while and I'd leave. Not caring about her screaming, hollering, and crying as I made my exit. I was always the type of nigga to give her some space for a couple days and then come back home when I thought she was over it.

No *"sorry"..."my bad"... "I'll do better"*. Nothing. So I never fully understood where Unc was coming from, and why he'd cared about my aunt's feelings so much. And then I met Kenya, my gangster.

She was currently looking down at me with glossy eyes. I could hear my own heart beating outside of my chest. I'd asked her why she was crying, and she refused to answer me. Instead, she looked away, quickly wiping a tear that dropped from her right eye.

Confused, I rose up from the floor and leaned over her. "Yo, Kenya, what's up?" I gripped her chin, making her face me. She didn't even wanna look at me. "What the fuck you–" I stopped mid-sentence when I felt a blow to my left eye. I closed both of my eyes for a second, trying to figure out what the fuck had just happened.

Did this bitch just hit me?

I opened my eyes, blinking them slowly, just as she hopped off the bed and sucker punched me dead in the side of the head. Before she could get another shot off, I grabbed her crazy ass by her arms.

"Let me go!" she yelled, trying to tug away from me. I gripped her arms tighter, slinging her onto the bed.

"What the fuck is wrong with you?!" I roared as she hopped out the bed.

"Fuck you, Cole. Dirty-dick-ass bitch!" she screamed; eyes red with tear-stained cheeks.

I gave her mental ass a confused look and she rushed me again.

"Yo, Kenya!" She hit me in my other eye. "Chill out!" I grabbed her forearms and she kneed me in the nuts.

"Bitch!" Before I could stop it, my hand came down hard on the side of her face. She stumbled back in a daze and I caught her before she hit the floor.

"Get off me!" she cried, snatching away from me. She began storming toward the bathroom.

Catching her mid stride, I wrapped my arms around her. "Baby, I'm sorry." I kissed the back of her neck. The Chinese symbol that she told me meant *loyalty*, stared back at me.

"Let me go, Cole." Her voice got hard. I still held on tight. "Let me gooooo." She broke down into a fit of tears.

"Baby, man...What the fuck?" My feelings were all conflicted and shit. I wanted to snap her fuckin' neck, but I needed to know why she was attacking me. Crying. I felt guilty for hitting her, but she kneed me in my nuts, so it felt justified. Kissing the side of her face where it was turning red, I held onto her like my life depended on it.

We stood there. I'm the middle of the room. Her crying...me confused. "Kenya, tell me something." I begged. "Talk to me ma."

She smacked her lips. "Go talk to the bitch that put them scratches on your back." She tried to sound tough, but her voice cracked and the tears started again.

Fuck. Remi...

"Baby, chill, man. It ain't even like that," I tried to reason with her.

"Just let me go, Cole." She tried pulling away.

"Can we at least talk about it?" I didn't know who this person was speaking for me, begging a bitch to hear him out.

"No." She gave up her fight for freedom and sobbed quietly in my chest.

"Baby, she don't mean shit to me," I told her. And I meant it. Remi was cool, but she wasn't Kenya.

She had me feeling like I was about to lose her. And I wasn't letting that shit happen. We'd been kicking it a lot, and without trying, she'd become a permanent fixture in my life. Her loud-ass laugh. Smart mouth. Even the way she threw her leg over me to fall asleep. I needed that. She couldn't just stop fuckin' with me. I wouldn't let her.

Since I'd met Kenya, I'd always been the one to come to her rescue. Make it better if possible. I'd kill anything moving if it caused her any type of pain or turmoil. So being the one responsible for her tears was tugging at my heart strings.

"I want to go back home, Cole," she demanded in a raspy whisper.

"Kenya, let me explain."

"Explain what?" Her voice iced over. I could feel her body tense up. "That you're fucking bitches in New York and fucking me too? No..." Her voice cracked. "Or do you want to explain to me why you disrespected me by letting the hoe scratch your back up?"

"She don't mean shit to me. I swear on everything." She had me sounding like a straight bitch. But I didn't give not one fuck. I was on the verge of losing something precious to me.

"Do you at least use condoms?"

"Come on now." I got offended. "You know I don't get down like that."

"How do I know? *We've* never used one," she shot back.

"On my daughter, I always strap up." Kenya had me putting shit on Tati's name. Yeah, she was stuck with me.

"How would you feel if I had sex with another man?" she asked. And even though it was hypothetical, I clenched my jaws. The thought of Kenya letting another nigga touch her body, explore what was rightfully mine, made me want to put her ass through a wall.

"You wouldn't do that," I answered.

"How do you know?"

"'Cause you're not stupid," I stated calmly. I had to remind myself she hadn't actually fucked another nigga so I needed to chill.

She scoffed. "It's not because I'm not stupid. It's because I care about you. I want to be with you. Only you. All these other niggas don't mean shit to me because they can't hold a candle to you."

The room became silent again.

"I...I love you, Cole. I have so much respect for you. I know you don't love me back, but I thought the respect was mutual."

"I do respect you."

She sighed. "Can we please just go? I just want to go home."

I felt like shit. I remembered the very first time I held her in my arms. She cried then. Now, here I was holding her for what might be the last time. Crying. This time because of my fuck up.

I guess you really do lose 'em how you get 'em.

Chapter Eleven

... I just want somebody ... to treat me like somebody

Kenya

Lying across Blaze's bed listening to the slow music seeping out of the Bluetooth speakers, it was like déjà vu. Only difference this time was I wasn't alone. Blaze lay at the bottom of the bed at my feet. I sniffled and she rubbed my leg.

"I hate him."

"I know," she replied sadly.

I'd been back in Missouri for two days and it was crazy how the weather matched my mood. Grey, gloomy...rainy. Looking down at my phone again, I sucked my teeth.

"That him again?"

"Yeah. I'm about to block his ass," I spat.

"You want me to have Kai talk to him?" she asked, sitting up.

"No. I just want him to leave me alone." How did he expect for me to get over him when he called me twenty times an hour.

"You want *me* to talk to him?"

"No." I sighed. What difference would it make?

"I can't believe he hit you. When I see him I got some words for his ass," she fussed.

"I hit him first. Repeatedly. And kneed him in the nuts." I found myself defending him.

"I mean, but damn. He couldn't just restrain you?"

"He tried."

"And what about the chick? Who is she?"

"I don't know. He said she wasn't important." I sat up straight. "But I know she lives in New York." That was a valuable piece of information. She was closer to Cole than I was.

Blaze got up from her bed and disappeared out of the room. I reached for my phone just as Cole was calling again. I contemplated on whether I should answer or not. What could he even say to me? *Sorry?* If so, he could keep his apologies. Ignoring his call yet again, I flopped back onto the bunch of pillows lined against Blaze's headboard.

"You hungry?" She entered the room holding three Pizza Hut boxes and a hot wing container on top.

My stomach growled my answer. I hadn't eaten since before I got drunk in Miami.

"What you get?" I rubbed my stomach.

"Umm...meatlovers, pepperoni, and three cheese." She sat the pizzas down on the comforter. "Oh! Yeah and...boneless buffalo wings." She plopped down next to me.

"Ooouuu ..." I rubbed my hands together. "I'm starving." Opening the box on top, I revealed the pepperoni pizza. My mouth watered as I lifted a piece out and put it to my lips. "Mmmm," I moaned catching a pepperoni that fell.

"So..." Blaze bit off of a hot wing. "What are you going to do about Cole? Are you completely done with him?" She reached for a slice of pizza.

"Hell yeah, I'm done with his cheating ass."

"Abusive too." Blaze chimed.

I rolled my eyes. "He's not abusive, Blaze." Of course I didn't approve of *any* man putting his hands on a woman. Which is why Cole had me fucked up. I was in no way trying to justify his reason for putting his hands on me, but in his defense, I attacked him. Repeatedly. I'm sure the final straw was when I tried to break his entire dick.

I chuckled inwardly, taking another bite. When I kneed him I wanted to make sure he never used his dick again. Just the thought of him putting what was mine in the next bitch, had me ready to grab one of his guns on the night stand and shoot his ass. He was lucky it was my knee that connected with his nuts and not a bullet.

"You said the same thing about Alonzo." Blaze put her crust down.

"Alonzo was different, so don't do that." I frowned. "What he did...used to do to me, Cole wouldn't." Cole would never hurt me intentionally. Yeah, he had a bad attitude, slight anger issues, but he never...he'd never put me in harm's way.

"Look, Kenya, I..." she huffed. "I didn't mean to make you feel some type of way just now." Blaze began to explain. "I just don't wanna see you hurt anymore." Her eyes danced around me. "It's just..."

"Blaze...I didn't come here to talk about Alonzo or Jamarcus, hell Cole neither." My voice rose an octave higher than I wanted it to, but I continued. "I came here to be around love. Support. I don't need you throwing my past in my face!"

"I get it. It's a touchy subject, Ken."

"No, Blaze you don't get it! Your perfect life and perfect fuckin' relationship. Perfect job. You don't get the hurt I've been through," I snapped, grilling her.

"Wow..." she shook her head, eyes holding a look of disbelief. "My life is perfect, Kenya? You've known me since third grade." She slipped off the bed and onto her feet. Pointing her index finger into her chest, she frowned. "*My* life is perfect?" she asked again.

I honestly didn't know what to say. Blaze was right, though. I'd known her my whole life. We'd laughed, joked, fought...cried together. The day her mother left a note and walked out of her life, Blaze cried in the bathroom for hours. We both did.

"Blaze—"

"Kenya..." with hurt written all over her face she continued, shaking her head. "What Alonzo did to you, I'm sorry." She blinked and the glossy look in her eyes didn't go unnoticed. "I wish I could've been there. I *should've* been there. But you can't take your anger out on me over something neither of us had control over." She paused to wipe her tears away. "You can't continue to go through life being angry. And it's not normal for a man to put his hands on you...and yours on him. That's not love, Ken."

I absentmindedly wiped the stream of tears from my cheeks. "You're right." I sniffled. "I'm just so fuckin' mad,

113

Blaze." I broke down and cried into my hands as I felt Blaze wrap her arms around me.

"I don't know what's wrong with me." I sobbed.

"There's nothing wrong with you, Kenya. Look at you. You're beautiful, smart, witty, and amazing," Blaze stressed, crying as well. "Don't let a man define who you are."

"But, Alonzo...Jarmarcus...Cole." I shook my head. "I just wanna be loved, Blaze. I wanna love somebody. And I want that same somebody to love me more."

Blaze

My heart bled listening to Kenya cry in my arms. My best friend was going through a lot. Not just with Cole, nor Jamarcus; her past still had a nasty hold on her, halting her from reaching her full potential. Squeezing her tighter, I wished I could take all her hurt and uncertainty about herself away. I wished she could see what I saw in her.

"I'm sorry, Blaze." She continued crying. "You've always been there for me. Looking out. You've always been my rock. I didn't mean..."

"It's okay, Ken," I assured her. Whether Kenya believed it or not, I got it. I understood the makings of her.

"Just hearing his name makes me sick to my stomach," she told me, still sobbing. "I hate him. I hate myself for giving him so much control over me."

I closed my eyes.

"I know it's not normal to fight in a relationship. I hate it." She sniffled. "I hate myself for making me and Jamarcus' relationship like that. I hate that I hit Cole."

I pulled her closer.

"Cole would never hit me first. I...it's just what I'm used to, so I lashed out," she admitted. "Alonzo...he's, he made me think that was normal. That's why I stayed with Jamarcus. Couples argue."

"But getting physical isn't normal, Kenya. The things Alonzo did, you thought were okay, because you were so much younger than him. He took advantage of you, baby. You were fourteen years old," I tried to reason with her.

I could feel her calming down. Her breathing became steady. "We were young, dumb, and hurt. Growing up too fast. But you've grown from that dark place, Kenya. He's gone. Alonzo can't hurt you anymore." I pulled away from her to look her in the face. "Just because you and Jamarcus had a physical relationship, doesn't mean it has to be that way with every man you encounter. You're better than that. You're a twenty-five-year-old college graduate and a public relations specialist for one of the most pristine companies in Missouri."

She nodded.

"You have a beautiful house...*Pearl.*" I said referring to her 2009 Honda Accord. "And most importantly me." I blinked away my tears. "I love you, Kenya. Blood couldn't make you more of a sister to me."

She gave a weak smile. "Thank you, Blaze."

"Anytime." I let her go to sit down on the bed.

We sat in a comfortable silence until Kenya's phone went off again. She looked down at it.

"Are you going to answer him?" Cole's name flashed across the screen.

"I don't know what to say to him." She watched it ring.

"He obviously has a lot to say to you. He's been calling all day." I smiled. I could tell Kenya was really feeling Cole. The little sparkle in her eye every time he came up gave it away. Good for her.

Kenya chuckled. "Annoying ass."

"Let him do all the talking," I offered. "Just hear what he has to say." It wasn't like they were in a relationship. Still, I understood where she was coming from. Cole was unofficially-officially hers. They were complicated like that.

"I told him I loved him." She sighed.

"Did you mean it?"

"I did. That's what made me go ballistic on his ass." She rolled her eyes to the back of her head.

"Did he say it back?"

"No. But I didn't tell him for him to say it back."

Her phone started ringing again.

"Answer the phone for that man. He's not letting you go."

Chapter Twelve

Mixed emotions

Cole

Holding my phone to my ear with my shoulder as I counted the stack of money in my hands, I waited for Kenya to answer. When it went to voicemail, I listened to her voice asking whoever was calling to leave a name and number and she'd call back. Kai sat down across from me at the table as the line beeped. Sighing, I shook my head at what the fuck I was about to do. Kenya had a nigga trippin'.

"Yo, Kenya, I know you see me callin' your stubborn ass." I paused, sitting the money down on the glass table. "Answer the phone, Ma. Matter fact, if you don't call me back in the next hour, I'm coming down to Missouri." Hanging up the phone, I sat it down and picked the stack back up.

"Shorty still ain't fuckin' with you?" Kai passed me the blunt he'd been puffing on.

Taking it, I put it to my lips, shaking my head. "Nah. Ima just shoot down to Missouri if she keep playing with me."

He nodded.

Just as my phone started ringing, the homies, Nasir and Quan, entered the dining room.

"What up?" Quan took a seat, followed by Nasir who gave a head nod to me and Kai.

"Shit, counting this paper up." I said, passing the blunt back to Kai.

"So we got word back on that nigga, Joey." Nasir leaned back in his chair.

My eyes shot up from the money in my hands. "And?"

"Some cat from North Philly." He reached for the blunt as Kai handed it to him.

"Philly?" I looked over at Kai. "Who we beefin' wit' in Philly?"

Kai leaned forward in his chair. "Philly? You sure?" He looked back and forth between Quan and Nasir.

Quan nodded. "Yeah...this bitch named Paige who Dre was fuckin' wit' said him and Joey was brothers. Shared the same father and shit." He took the blunt from Nasir, and Kai lit another one.

Kai frowned. "Dre wasn't no Philly nigga, though."

"Apparently, he moved up here with his mother," Nasir cut in. "We paid her a little visit earlier today." He smirked.

"So where is Joey?" Kai started texting on his phone. "What is his father's name?"

I sat the money down. "Tell me where I can find these niggas." My trigger finger was itching.

"Paige said Joey been in hiding ever since Dre disappeared. The father is some old head named Big Moe." Quan removed his phone from his pocket. "Government name is Maurice Gardener. Hold most of Philly down. Been holding for a minute."

I stood, snatching my burner up. "A'ight. Let's go ride down on this nigga."

Nasir stood up as well.

Kai raised his left hand telling us to chill. "Quan, continue."

"Continue?" I looked down at Kai. "Fuck is you talkin' 'bout? I don't need to hear no more."

"Yo, Cole, chill. Quan, go ahead."

Quan chuckled. "You niggas is wild," he stated, referring to me and Nasir. "But check it." He leaned forward, placing his elbows on the table. "That nigga, Big Moe, ain't feelin' you at all, Kai. Since you been outta prison, you been taking shit over. Word is niggas from Philly been copping weight up here."

"So you know niggas mad," Nasir cosigned.

"What the fuck that gotta do with me?" I seethed. Niggas was tryna take me out and over what? *Jealousy*?"

Quan continued, "We went down to Philly just to hear what word on the street was." He sighed. "Niggas is talkin'."

"Sayin' Kai money ain't letting niggas eat unless they rollin' wit' him." Nasir faced me. "Talkin' 'bout how flashy you are. Buying new whips every other month and shit. They know we gettin' money."

"Big Moe got a team of soldiers keeping him protected and shit. His estate got like six goons just walkin' the perimeter."

"Pussy-ass nigga..." I sat back down.

"So what's the next move?" Quan looked to Kai.

"I'm tryna put niggas in body bags." I placed my gun on the table.

"I heard that." Nasir relit the blunt.

"Say less." Kai picked up a stack.

Blaze

Looking at the time on my phone, I saw it was almost ten. I hadn't spoken to Mehkai in almost the entire day. I'd called him numerous times, but to no avail. It usually wasn't like him to go so long without calling or checking in. And he knew how I felt about that.

Mehkai's fast lifestyle made my nerves bad. I constantly worried about him and his well-being. To me, it was like he was playing Russian roulette with his own life. I looked down at my phone again. The thought of Mehkai being hurt immediately put me in my feelings. How would I live without him? I couldn't. My heart...my heart couldn't bare it.

"Damn it, Mehkai." I blew out an exasperated breath. Sitting in front of the large sketchbook on my easel, I started shading in pieces of my work.

Where is he?

Eight. That's how many times I'd called him. I didn't want to hound him, but I needed to know he was alive and okay. I needed to hear his voice.

With my pencil still in my right hand, I picked my phone up with my left. The screen was already on his contact information because I'd been calling him all day.

Before I could press the icon to call him, again, an incoming call from him appeared on the screen. I smiled.

"I was just about to blow your phone up."

He chuckled lightly. "Ah yeah?"

"Yeah. I missed you today." I wanted to ask where the hell he'd been, but I didn't want to ruin the moment. In all honesty, I was just happy my baby was all right.

"I missed you too, Ma."

"I can't tell."

"What are you doing?" He curved my comment.

"Drawing."

"Drawing what?"

"A portrait of Kenya. She's been kind of down lately."

"She straight?"

"No. Did you know Cole hit her?" I asked with an attitude.

"Nah, I ain't know that."

"Well, he did. Left a big, red mark on her face."

"Stay out of that," he told me before talking to somebody in his background.

"Kenya's my best friend. I'm not okay with him smacking her." I didn't care who hit who first or why. No real man should put his hands on a woman. Cole had lost major cool points with me.

"What did I just say?" Kai's deep voice held an authoritative tone. I didn't answer, I continued shading instead. "Let them work that out, a'ight?" He removed some of the bass out of his voice. Some.

"Whatever. Where have you been all day?" The mood was now ruined.

"Handling business."

"So you haven't seen me calling you? You couldn't check in? No text to let me know you were still breathing?" I rambled off question after question.

"I wasn't by my phone, Ma. Yo, Ava, go tell Cole and Nasir I'm 'bout to bounce."

I sat my pencil down. *Ava? Who the hell is Ava?* Frowning, I tilted my head the side slightly.

"Okay. Did you need anything else before I left?" Whoever she was, responded.

"Nah, shorty. Be safe."

"Later, Kai." I listened to her make her exit.

"Who is *Ava*, Mehkai?"

"Nobody."

"You know what?" I tittered in disbelief. I couldn't even get a phone call or text. His woman. Yet he had a bitch all in his face, asking if he *needed* anything.

"Yo, Blaze, don't start."

"You couldn't pick up the phone to call me, though? Mehkai, who the fuck is Ava's overly-friendly ass?" I snapped. "And what in the hell could you possibly *need* from her?" I hated how easy it was for him to put me in my feelings.

"She's the crew's assistant, Blaze." He sounded irritated with the conversation. With me.

"Assistant? You really expect me to believe that?"

"Then don't," he stated calmly. "I didn't call you to argue."

"But you called for me to hear another woman in your background?" I asked in disbelief.

"She was leaving."

"Why is she there?!" I yelled.

"I told you why." His voice still held that same calmness that was starting to annoy me.

"Is she why you couldn't answer for me all day?" I asked. Feelings crushed.

What is this man doing to me?

I could hear him suck his teeth. "Yo, if Kenya 'bout to start rubbing off on you, you coming to New York for a couple days. I got a lot of shit on my plate right now. I don't need no insecure bullshit from you right now, Ma."

The phone went silent. I'd never been the insecure type. But then again, I'd never had feelings for a man like Mehkai. He had me all out of my element. I wanted to ask him more about Ava. How long had she been there? What did she look like?

My heart rate sped up. What if he was attracted to her? Had they sexed? I didn't like the way he called her *shorty*. Why was it any of her business if he *needed* anything. I held onto my chest.

Am I having a panic attack? The phone went silent as I got my breathing together. Heart racing at the thought of another woman touching him. Him touching her in places that he touches me. Giving her the same kind of attention he gives me.

"Baby."

I blew out a deep breath. "What, Kai?" I was officially in my feelings.

"I told you there ain't nobody else but you. Ava is a homie."

I thought she was your assistant.

"We have a business-only relationship. She don't even get down like that."

Oh...so you're defending her. I rolled my eyes.

"You hear me?"

"I hear you, Kai."

"Stop pouting." I heard him shut the car door.

"I'm not."

"I'll call you and wrap with you tomorrow, a'ight?"

"Do I have a choice?" I asked with a little too much attitude. I'm sure Mehkai wasn't feeling me at all.

"Yo, Blaze, I'll see you later."

"Whatever."

He hung up and I pulled the phone away from my face.

***

The next morning...around 8:30ish.

"Hello?" I mumbled into the phone receiver. I didn't know what time it was, but I knew it was early. And I was tired.

"Is this Blaze?" a woman asked.

I looked over at the clock on my nightstand. "Who is this?"

"Ava. I'm Kai's assistant." She paused waiting for my response.

However, I didn't give her one. Instead, I hung up the phone. *Kai got me fucked up on so many levels.* I pressed my screen a few times before putting the phone back to my ear.

"Lil Mama..." The sound of his voice made me shiver.

"Really? You got females calling me?" Kai having Ava call me to prove she was his assistant made it look even more suspect.

"Blaze, you on one for real." He sighed. "What she say?"

"She asked who I was, then said she was your *assistant.*" I sat up straight. It was too early for this bullshit.

"And what did you tell her?"

Is he serious right now?

"Blaze!"

"I hung up on her!"

"Why?"

"Kai, you are really testing me. You wanna keep—"
My sentence was cut short when I noticed there was no

sound on his end. I pulled my phone away from my face and saw he'd hung up on me. *No he didn't.*

I started to call him back just as a New York number flashed across my screen.

His phone must've died.

"Mehkai, you—"

"Blaze, please don't hang up on me. This is Ava," she rushed her sentence out.

"What do you want?"

"Kai told me to call and let you know your flight leaves at ten."

"What flight?" I asked, annoyed.

"Your flight to New York." When I didn't reply, she continued. "He said not to pack anything." She held a thick New York accent. "He told me to tell you to just grab your purse and go to the airport once you're dressed." The wind whistled in my ear letting me know she was outside somewhere.

"Tell Mehkai to kiss my ass." I got comfortable underneath my covers. I was going back to sleep.

She laughed. "Umm, Blaze, he said if you're not here by three, he's putting you in the doghouse."

I frowned. "Excuse me?"

"He said if you can't follow simple instructions, you'll regret it. His words," she clarified.

Kai had me so fucked up.

"Look, Blaze." She cleared her throat. "Kai must like you a lot. He's never had me do this before. Girl, he got me planning a flight, spa day, and a shopping spree. I wasn't supposed to tell you all that, but I can tell you're not really feeling me."

I looked over at the clock on my night stand again.

"What better way to be mad at him, than by spending all his money?"

I chuckled quietly at her.

"I say you come to New York, be pampered, and shop till you drop. Your plane ticket is first class, and you don't have to bring nothing but your purse and the clothes on your back." She continued to try and buy me. "Plus Kai's not easy to deal with when he doesn't get his way." She paused.

I rolled my eyes. I mean, I did miss my baby, which I knew was part of the reason I'd been so moody with him. The trip was paid for and I didn't have to haul any luggage.

Peeling the covers back from my body, I sighed into the phone. "Ten?"

"I'll text you the information."

130

Chapter Thirteen

Straight to it

Kenya

This cannot be happening.

I flipped the box over to make sure I was reading it right. Skimming through the instructions, I groaned. *No...no.* I closed my eyes and hung my head in disappointment. Throwing the box in the small trash can next to the toilet, I began unraveling tissue to wipe.

"Kenya," I started chastising myself. "You know better."

Flushing the toilet, I stood up and wrapped my silk robe around me. Washing my hands, I then dried them off as I stared at my reflection in the mirror. My new twenty-four-inch Peruvian bundles I'd had Kayla install yesterday were pulled up into a messy bun. No makeup on and my Nike prescription glasses sat on my nose. My already light complexion looked drained and tired.

That's all I'd been doing lately anyway. Sleeping. At first I thought it was because my menstrual was about to come down, especially since I'd been cramping. But when I checked my calendar, it showed I was two weeks late for *this* month. Then I flipped the calendar back and I saw I hadn't gotten one last month at all.

I'd taken twelve pregnancy tests. *Twelve.* And each time they came back positive, I thought God was playing a mean trick on me. I couldn't blame anyone but myself, though. Cole and I hadn't used a condom *ever*. I figured my birth control pills would do the trick. They always did when I was with Jamarcus.

Turning off the light, I made my exit. I almost reached my room when there was loud banging on my front door. Immediately, I assumed it was Cole. I replayed the voicemail he'd left on my phone five days ago, about twenty times. Just to hear his voice.

I never called back. Didn't intend on it. The feelings I had for Cole scared the shit out of me. Too afraid to love him, terrified of losing him. And yet still he had my heart.

Reaching the door, I gripped the handle. "Who is it?"

"It's Amina, bitch. Open the door. It's cold out here," my older sister cursed.

Breathing a sigh of relief, I opened the door and let her in. "Hey. What are you doing here?"

She walked in carrying my nephew on her hip. "I was in the neighborhood. What you cook?" she asked, putting him down.

"Nothing. I was actually going to call Blaze and see if she wanted to meet up." I shrugged and shut the door.

"Ugh." She smacked her lips. Amina was fake as hell. Whenever Blaze was around she treated her like a little sister. Or at least tried. But as soon as she wasn't around, she acted like she couldn't tolerate her.

"Ugh what?"

"Nothing. We can go out to eat. I need to tell you about my stupid-ass baby daddy." She removed my nephew's coat and then hers.

Rolling my eyes, I headed back upstairs to my room with her on my heels. Amina's baby daddy was supposedly some guy named Santonio. She claimed they were in a relationship, but I'd never met him. I do recall helping her fight in the club over him. She needed to leave his ass alone.

"What did he do?" I asked as we entered my room.

"He's just getting on my damn nerves. He's still saying Santana's not his."

I stopped mid-way to the closet to look at her. "Well, is he?" I'd never met him, and he didn't even show up to the hospital when my nephew was born. It just didn't add up.

"Bitch. You tried it." She waved me off, taking a seat on my bed.

"I'm just saying." I continued to my closet.

"Don't then."

"Whatever." I stepped into my walk-in closet.

"You wanna watch cartoons?" she asked my nephew and I could hear my television come on.

Reaching inside of my robe for my phone, I pulled up Blaze's number and sent her a quick text.

Me: B! We need to talk asap. Link up tonight?

Then scrolling down to Cole's name, I let my thumb hover over the call icon. Poking my head back into the bedroom, I noticed my nephew was sitting in the middle of the bed and Amina was gone. Shutting the closet door, I called him and waited for him to answer. When I got his voicemail, I waited for the beep. Taking a deep breath, I licked my lips and I leaned against my wall of jeans.

"Cole, I was just calling to talk to you. I..." I contemplated on whether or not I should hang up. "Cole, I'm pregnant."

Kai

"Did she land yet?" I held my phone to my ear as Cole pulled into a parking spot.

Ava giggled. "I'm at the airport now, boss man. I'll text you when I get her, okay?" She tried to rush me off the phone.

"As soon as you see her shoot me a text, Ava."

"Kai, okay. And don't be blowing my phone up. I got this. I got her. Don't ruin our fun by being a bug-a-boo." She laughed. But I knew she was dead ass.

"A'ight. Hit my line if she need anything."

"Bye, Kai. Talk to you later."

I knew Blaze would have an attitude when Ava told her I was in Philadelphia. But I had some shit to take care of. As long as she was at my condo when I got home, then I was straight. Ava planned a lot of girly shit to keep her preoccupied until then. Right now, I had scores to settle. Beef to handle.

First mission was to find Joey. Like Nasir said though, the streets talk. That's why we were sitting outside of

135

Dreams, a strip joint located in Old City. Cole double-checked the silencer on the two glocks sitting on his lap as Quan and Nasir pulled next to us. Checking out the scenery, I was glad to see nobody was outside. It was almost two-thirty on a Wednesday, so I was sure everyone was at work. Well, everybody besides that nigga Joey and the crew of six nigga he was rollin' with.

Sliding my hands into my burner gloves, I made sure they were secure. Opening the glove compartment, I removed the Chucky mask I'd bought in Atlanta a couple of months ago.

"Nigga, you a psycho." Cole grinned, slipping a Michael Myers mask over his face.

Once my mask was on, I reached down on the floor for my AK. I opened my door the same time Nasir opened his driver's door. He gave me a quick head nod, wearing a clown mask. Tec-9 in hand, Quan approached our side of the car carrying two Rugers with a Scream mask covering his face.

Cole and Nasir left the cars running as we headed to the entrance of the building. It was broad daylight, but we were on a murder mission. The club's bouncer wasn't standing outside, so Cole rushed in first. Crashing a bottle girl in the side of her head with the handle of his gun, she hit the floor and we rushed in past him.

Me, Cole, and Nasir split up, while Quan held down the exit. Bitches were screaming and shit, but I ain't give a fuck. Everybody had to die. Joey and his homies jumped up and went reaching for their heats, but the mirage of our different bullets lit their section up. One by one, they hit the floor.

A bullet whizzed by my face, but I dodged it. Running quickly behind a wall, I let off another round, shooting some dread-head nigga in the face.

"Aaaagh!" A woman crouched down underneath a table next to me hollered. "Please..." she begged. "Please...please. I have a son. Please don't kill me," she cried with snot running down her face.

"Fuck!" somebody yelled by Joey's section.

Taking my focus off ole girl, I hurriedly emptied my clip into some fat nigga behind the bar. The gun he had aimed at Cole dropped on the counter. Cole nodded my way as a small group of females rushed to the exit. I knew Quan would handle that.

Soon, the only sound in the joint was Big Sean's "Paradise" blaring from the speakers. Oh...and the snotty nosed bitch under the table still begging for her life. Snatching her up, I tossed her out into the open floor. Still screaming and crying, Nasir ended that with one hit to the head, though.

We quickly parted ways to sweep the club out. Once I was positive nobody was in the bathroom or locker room, I headed back to the front. Meeting back at the entrance with Cole and Nasir, we all rushed outside hopping into the stolen whips. Cole sped off down the street, and Nasir went the opposite direction.

***

Forty minute later, we all pulled up at the same time in the back of an abandoned warehouse in Georgetown. Cole put the car in park before he hopped out and rushed to the trunk. I quickly removed the mask from my face, followed by the black hoodie I was wearing. I tossed them into the back seat next to my AK. Opening my door, I stepped out into the cold, removing the black T-shirt I had on.

Cole came to my side, handing me a black duffel bag. Grabbing it from him, I walked off to change my clothes.

Cole

"Is that everything?" I asked, making sure anything that could connect us to a crime scene was in one of the whips.

"Down to my socks."

"Yo, get rid of them whips. Shit, y'all know what to do." I listened to Kai give out orders.

They nodded.

"When you get back to the city, stay low." He looked directly at Nasir who had a smug grin on his face. "We'll meet up at the spot in a couple hours."

"A'ight."

We all gave each other daps before Nasir and Quan hopped in the separate black Buick Century's. The tinted windows were just as black as the cars.

Kai followed me to my Camaro and hopped in. "Make sure you check with them niggas," he instructed, lighting a blunt then taking a hard hit.

"Them nigga ain't new to this." I pulled off. "But I got you." He handed me the weed.

After reaching in my console for my phone, I saw I had several missed calls. The only one that caught my attention was the one from Kenya. I smiled. She finally decided to call a nigga back. I had stopped trying to reach her a few days ago.

Stubborn ass.

Hopping on the expressway, I handed the blunt back to Kai who was shaking his head at his phone.

"Blaze spoiled ass gon' make me hem her ass up," he vented, taking a pull.

I laughed. "Giggles got you over there in your feelings.

He waved me off and smirked, shaking his head. Giggles was a good look for my nigga.

Glancing down at my phone once again, a voicemail notification from Kenya showed. Clicking on it, I put the phone to my ear and waited to hear her cuss me out for not answering. I licked my lips as the message started. She was talking low...stalling on what she was trying to say. I knew why she was hesitating when the message finally ended.

Cole, I'm pregnant.

Chapter Fourteen

... Brooklyn...

Blaze

I sat in the passenger seat of Ava's pink Bentley texting Mehkai. Why the hell would he send for me, and then leave out of the state? Since Ava had picked me up from the airport almost an hour ago, I'd called him *and* texted him, which he didn't answer. I was pissed. He had me riding through *his* city with a chick I didn't know.

Ava was cool for the most part. She'd taken me to a nice little diner to get something to eat. And we'd just left the liquor store so she could make drinks at her house. She was gorgeous like I knew she would be. Standing at maybe five foot six, her mocha skin was vibrant and blemish free. She had the same pouty lips as Meagan Good and her cat-like eyes were dark grey. Her jet black pixie cut was tapered to perfection on both sides. The shiny diamond medusa piercing above her upper lip sparkled each time the sun hit. Ava was beautiful.

I looked down at my phone just as Mehkai texted me.

My baby: have you ate

Me: when are you coming back?

My baby: when I get there

Me: really Kai?

My baby: go have fun and quit pouting ima get wit you later aight

I reread the message...frowning.

"Ok...we're here." Ava put her car in park. "You ready to get fucked up?" She cheesed, reaching into the backseat for the bags holding the alcohol.

"I guess." I sighed reading Mehkai's message again.

"Cheer up, we're about to kick it. My girl Ryan is coming through, so we 'bout to be lit." She said getting out of the car.

Oh hell no.

I rolled my eyes getting out. I didn't hang around females, and for good reasons. They were catty, jealous, messy and just plain *extra*. Ever since our little small chat at the bar a couple weeks ago, my neighbor Cassandra had been trying to get me to hang out with her and her twin sister. Each time I declined. I was good with Kenya. She was all the female friend I could handle anyway.

Ava must've sensed the distain on my face, causing her to laugh. "You sure you're not from New York?" She asked as we made our way up the stairs to her Brownstone.

I shook my head. "Why you ask that?"

"Because, you got that New York around the way girl attitude." She fumbled with her keys.

"You need help?" I grabbed one of the paper bags out of her arms.

"Thank you." She smiled, pushing the front door open.

"You're welcome." I followed her inside, shutting the door behind me.

"Make yourself comfortable, Blaze. Ryan should be on her way in a little bit. She said she was crossing the bridge." Ava sashayed to her kitchen with me close behind.

"Yeah...about that." I sat the bag I was carrying down on the kitchen island. "Randy might be cool and all, but I don't just hang with females I don't know. No offense." I shrugged as she went into the refrigerator. Lesson learned.

She came back out with two bottles of water. "None taken. And her name is Ryan." She smiled handing me a bottle. "You'll love her."

"I doubt it," I mumbled retrieving my phone from my oversized MCM bag. Going into the dining room, I sat down at the mahogany table.

Looking around her home, I complimented the bright yellow and white she'd done it in. The plush yellow sofa popped well with the splashes of powder blue from her couch pillows, curtains, and floor rug. It was a little too loud for my taste, but it was cute. The huge blue vase on her dining room table held at least two dozen sunflowers and a few white lilies. Giving the room an airy look.

Clicking on the text message from Kenya, I saw she needed to talk asap.

Me: cant meet up. in New York, I'll tell you about it later. everything ok?

I pressed send just as Ava entered the room holding two glasses.

"Put that phone down, ma'am." She laughed sitting a glass in front of me. "Kai got you all in love."

I chuckled. "Ain't nobody worried about Mehkai."

"Mmhm, tell me anything." She sat down and there was a knock on the front door. "Come in!"

The door pushed open, and in walked a beautiful chick with long, pink hair. "The party has arrived!" she grinned shutting the door with her foot. I then noticed the many bags she was carrying.

"Just in time. I just finished making the drinks. Let me go get yours." Ava stood up, going back into the kitchen.

"You must be Blaze." She dropped the bags. "Ryan..." She extended her hand.

Accepting her handshake, I smiled. "Nice to meet you."

Taking her parka off, she revealed two arms full of colorful tattoos. "So you're the one Kai Money all in love with." She beamed, showcasing her pretty white teeth.

"I wouldn't say in love." I giggled, picking my glass up.

"Bitch, please." She sat down and Ava came back. "That nigga got Ava planning you spa days and shopping sprees. The pussy must be fire!" She and Ava slapped fives.

"Okay!" Ava cosigned, sitting Ryan's glass in front of her.

I laughed. "Y'all stupid."

"I mean, he did good." Ryan took a hefty sip out of her glass. Ava nodded and she continued. "You're pretty as fuck. Got a banging-ass body. All you missing is a few tattoos." She winked at me.

I shook my head at her. Ryan was cool as hell.

"No." Ava disagreed. "Tattoos give you a hard look. You see my skin?" She rubbed her milk chocolate arms. "Flawless." She boasted, picking her cup up.

Ryan rolled her eyes. "Whatever. Quan loves them."

Ava stuck her tongue out at her.

"Quan?" I asked, sipping from my glass.

"Ryan's boo thaaang," Ava sang, smiling at Ryan.

Ryan smacked her lips, waving her off. "Quan's ass is in the dog house."

"Kind of like Blaze would've been if she hadn't gotten on that plane." Ava laughed and finished off her drink.

"Whatever." I tittered, finishing my drink as well.

A text alert from Kenya came through.

Ken: New York! have fun chica we'll talk later.

"Look, he blowing that ass up now." Ava stood up collecting everyone's glass.

"Actually, that was my homegirl. Mehkai ain't thinking about me." I pouted playfully. Whatever Ava mixed in those glasses was kicking in.

"Ohhh, boo boo," Ryan pouted too.

"I know. He get on my nerves," I huffed.

"That's men for you, especially paid, fine niggas. They think the world revolves around their arrogant asses." Ryan vented running her hands through her wavy hair.

Ava entered the room with refills for everybody. "Y'all in here male bashing for real," she joked, sitting the glasses down.

Reaching for mine, I nodded my head. "I feel you, Ryan. It's like you have to move on their time."

"Right." She sipped out of her glass.

"Y'all better leave my brothers alone," Ava warned, picking her glass up.

Ryan waved her off. "Tell your brother to leave me alone then. Quan swear I'm where he wanna be, but I'm fighting bitches every other week. I'm getting tired of the shit." I smiled at her, she reminded me of Kenya. Same high yellow complexion and everything.

"Don't get me started." Ava rolled her eyes. "He still ain't forgave me for telling you about that bitch he bought that bag for."

I frowned. *I wish the fuck Kai would.* Yeah, the liquor was definitely kicking in.

Ryan scoffed. "He irritates the hell out of me. He mad annoying."

147

"At least he ain't as bad as Cole's ignorant ass." Ava shook her head.

At the mention of Cole's name, I took a sip from my glass. *Yes, bitch, give me all the tea.*

Ryan shrugged. "He came to Miami with some pretty-ass bitch. I mean *bad*. Hair laid, body on point with pretty eyes. His ass was chasing her around like a lost puppy." She chuckled.

"Oh yeah...ummm" Ava snapped her fingers. "What was her name?"

"Kenya," I blurted. "My sister," I clarified.

Ava nodded. "Yeah. I liked her she seemed pretty cool. I didn't really get to hang with her, though. The guys had me with them." She sighed.

"She was mad cool." Ryan finished off her drink.

"Yeah, that's my baby." I smiled.

"She should've come. We're going to the mall after we leave here. She could've spent up all of Cole's money." Ryan slid her glass across the table to Ava. "Refill pleeease." She cheesed like a big kid.

I finished my drink off as well and pushed my glass toward Ava, grinning.

"Oh shit...hold on let me catch up." Ava chugged her drink down.

"Blaze, you know how to roll?" Ryan pulled a bag of marijuana out of her pink purse.

Chapter Fifteen

I miss you

Cole

As soon as I crossed the threshold of my townhouse, I was calling Kenya. I couldn't even bask in the events of my day. A nigga needed a drink. ASAP. She answered as I made my way behind my glass bar.

"Hello?"

My dick jumped. I don't know if it was because it had been awhile, but her voice was doing something to me. Made me forget all about the drink I was supposed to be making.

"What up, Ma? Long time no speak." The last time we'd had a conversation was back in Miami when she tried to beat me up. I chuckled.

"I know, right?" She sighed. "How have you been?"

"Straight. Making a few moves here and there. How you feeling?" I asked, referring to my seed she was carrying.

"Tired."

"Ah yeah? Get used to it." I smirked, going around to the front of the bar to take a seat on one of the stools.

"Cole."

"Yeah, Ma?"

"I can't keep this baby."

I stood back up to fix my drink. "How you figure that?"

"We're not even together. Hell, we're not even on speaking terms. How do you expect for us to co-parent?" I could hear noise in her background. "Stop, nephew."

"That's your fault." I snorted, pouring a double shot of D'usse.

"Whatever, Cole..."

"So you don't wanna have my baby, Kenya?" On some true shit, I dealt with bitches on a daily trying to trap me. In the past two years, I'd participated in six paternity tests. Call me arrogant, but I was surprised Kenya didn't want to be tied to me for life.

"Hell no."

I chuckled.

"Cole, I don't want to be just another one of your baby mamas."

I took the first shot. "Yo, Kenya, let's address what the real issue is." I threw the second shot back. "You still

151

mad about that shit in Miami. I get it, Ma. I fucked up. But how am I supposed to fix shit if you won't talk to me, huh?"

"Cole, I'm not even tripping about that no more," she lied. "I'm more concerned about the baby I'm carrying."

"So you don't love me no more?" Nah. I hadn't forgot.

"Cole..."

"Yes or no." I poured another set of shots. "You still in love wit' a nigga or what?"

"That's doesn't even matter." She tried to blow me off.

"Yo, look." I took a shot. "I'm sorry, shorty. It was mad disrespectful for me to let that bitch scratch my back up," I apologized. Something I was okay with doing only for Kenya. "You forgive Daddy?"

"Did you use a condom, Cole?"

"Do you forgive me?"

"Answer my question."

"Answer mine."

"Which one?"

"The first one."

"Yes, I forgive you." She sucked her teeth. And knowing shorty, she was probably rolling them pretty-ass eyes too.

"Nah, the one before that."

"What was it?" She tried to play dumb.

"You still love me?"

"Why does that matter?"

"'Cause I wanna know." For some strange reason. I *needed* to know.

"And if I said yes, what would that change?"

"Ain't shit changed between us, Kenya. You still my baby. Mad and all. The only reason I ain't been down to Missouri is because shit been hectic up here."

Again, she smacked her lips.

"You mad at me. I'll let you have that. Like I said, I fucked up."

"Okay."

I licked my lips. "I know you still love me. You aint even gotta answer the question." Taking a seat at the bar again, I checked the messages in my second phone.

"I still think I should get an abortion, Cole."

"Then you thinking too hard. Didn't we just make up?"

"No."

I smiled, shaking my head at her evil ass. "You right. It ain't official until I drop this dick off up in you."

"You live in New York and I live in Missouri. That wouldn't be fair to the baby."

"That's why you moving out here."

"Yeah fuckin' right."

"Quit cussin' in front of my baby."

"Boy, please. Cole, I'm serious. This is serious."

"Yo, Kenya, dead that abortion shit. You knew the possibilities of getting knocked up when you let me smash raw." I was slowly getting irritated with her bullshit.

"It's *my* body, Cole. I have the final decision on what I want to do in the end," she snapped back.

"Is that what you think?"

"That's what I *know*."

"A'ight." I nodded. "Check it, Ma. If you go through with an abortion and you kill my seed, I'ma murk your stupid ass." All that nice guy shit wasn't seeming to get through to her.

"Did you just threaten me?"

"Nah. That was a muthafuckin promise." I stood up. "Aye, I'm about to take a nap. Answer the phone when I call, Kenya."

"And if I don't?"

"I see them pregnancy hormones getting to you early." I chuckled, climbing the stairs.

"Whatever bye!" she yelled, hanging up in my face and shit.

I had half a mind to call her back and bite down on her little mean ass. But that wouldn't solve nothing. She'd still have that funky-ass attitude. And she'd still have me fucked up. That was a'ight, though. I had something for her.

My text alert went off as I laid across my bed on my back.

Remi: can u drop by ???

I licked my lips. I hadn't smashed her thick ass in almost three days. Replying back to her message, I sat up straight. A nigga deserved some pussy. And I knew just where to get it.

Chapter Sixteen

Winners never lose

Blaze

girl you workin' wit' some ass yeah
Ya bad yeah...
Make a nigga spend his cash yeah...
His last yeah..

"Aye!" Ryan jumped up from her seat. Dancing in place, she bent over, slightly twerking her butt.

I laughed, sipping from my straw, dancing in my seat. Since Ava had so much clout for rollin' with Mehkai and his crew, we were sitting in a lavish, burgundy VIP area. The bottles kept coming, and I'd even had a guy from the bar send me a drink. Ava and Ryan thought it was hilarious. I however, rolled my eyes and politely declined it.

Men were flocking to our area and not one could enter. Ava didn't care. Ryan on the other hand was too afraid to test Quan's gangster. I joked about how he had her on lock, but I could relate. There was no way I was going to allow word about a bunch of guys kicking it in our VIP get back to Mehkai.

Not including our pregame at Ava's house; I was about six drinks, five shots, and four blunts in. And I was definitely feeling myself. It was cold outside, so I wore dark distressed jeans, a white long sleeved, back out bodysuit, and gold *Guiseppe Zanotiti's* on my feet. Big, gold hoop earrings hung freely on each side of my face, hitting my cheeks every time I made a sharp turn. My makeup was bold, giving me a sexy sultry look. And my hair was pulled up into a tight, slick bun.

"Girl, this muthafucka is lit!" Ava pulled her dress down. "I'm getting me some dick tonight."

I shook my head, sipping from my straw again.

"Girrrl," Ryan slurred, plopping down next to me. "It's hot as hell in here."

"Sit your fast ass down then!" I giggled, bumping her playfully with my elbow.

She danced in her seat. "I'm fuckin' the shit out of DaQuan tonight." Sticking her tongue out, she started grinding in her seat.

"Ew nasty." Ava frowned. Like she hadn't *just* said she was leaving with somebody's son.

I laughed.

"Matter fact...what time is it?" Ryan picked her phone up off the table.

"Damn...it's already three-thirty..." She sighed.

"No it's not!" I grabbed for her phone. Ryan was drunk. There was no way it could be that late. My eyes shot to the time on the screen. *3:36am.*

"Let me text Quan. Where the fuck is he at?" I handed her phone back to her.

"Umm...no need." Ava looked down at us. "He and Nasir are coming this way."

"What?!" Ryan hopped, up looking past Ava.

I stood up too, hoping to see Mehkai. I didn't see him, and I didn't even know who Nasir and Quan were. I quickly figured it out though, when two fine-ass men approached the VIP rope. The first one entered talking on the phone while the second, who I assumed was Quan, swaggered over to Ryan. He lifted her up, hugging her tight.

"You know what time it is?" He put her down. "Your ass needs to be at home."

"What for?" She pulled on her long, silky, pink ponytail. "It ain't like you'd be there waiting on me."

He smirked and then looked over at me. "Who we got here?"

Ryan wrapped her left arm around my shoulders. "This is Blaze, Kai Money's, wife." She beamed.

I shook my head at her. "Girl please." I laughed, holding my hand out to him. "Nice to finally meet the man Ryan's been talking about all day."

He shook his head, grinning at her.

"That's how you do me, Blaze?" She tittered, wrapping her arms around his neck.

"You missed Daddy, huh?" He licked his lips.

"Yep!" Ava cosigned after drinking from the Hennessy bottle she was holding.

"Shut up." Ryan kissed his lips.

"Ayo, Blaze, right?" The other guy I'm guessing was Nasir asked me.

"Yeah...Nasir?" I extended my hand.

"Yeah." He shook it. "That nigga, Kai, outside waiting on you."

"Really?" I'm sure my face lit up at the mention of my baby.

"Yeah. I'll walk you out." He took off toward the exit.

"Aw man..." Ava pouted. "You hoes is dick whipped."

159

Ryan gave Quan a dreamy look. "Don't be hatin'."

***

I somehow managed to follow Nasir out of the club and outside without falling. I kept blinking like that would help my blurred vision. I'm sure I was swaying as I tried to keep up with his long strides. The cold air helped me come to. Just a little. Holding on tight to my clutch, I walked past a group of party goers.

"That's the ugly bitch I was tellin' you about, Syn. The one that's fuckin' Mehkai." The mention of Kai's name made me stop in my tracks.

"Yeah, hoe, I'm talkin' to you." I turned to see who was talking so reckless. When my eyes locked on hers, an instant frown graced my face. Monique.

"Yo, bitch, who the fuck you talkin' to?" Nasir stopped.

"Fuck you, Nasir," she snapped; hands on her shapely hips.

I blinked and Nasir drew his gun from his hip and pointed it at her. "Say what?" he asked.

"Nas—"

"Nah, bitch. Say what you just said."

Monique backed up.

"Yo, Nas!" Mehkai's deep voice reminded me I needed to breathe. "Chill."

Nasir chuckled. "I ain't gon' shoot you, bitch." Monique looked terrified. "Ayo, I'ma rap wit' you later, Kai Money." He threw deuces up over his shoulder before heading back into the club.

"Come on, Ma." Mehkai grabbed my hand.

I looked back at Monique, who had a crowd of women surrounding her. "Maybe you should go check on her," I offered as he grabbed the small of my back, helping me into the passenger's seat of his G-Wagon.

"You drunk as fuck. Get in, Ma," he urged me. Once I was in, he closed the door.

"Why are you this drunk?" He asked as soon as he was in the SUV. "You can barely stand up straight and shit," He chastised me.

"Mehkai, where have you been?" I slurred, turning in my seat. I hadn't spoken to him since I'd first touched down in New York.

"Out taking care of business. You high too?" He stopped at a red light, looking over at me. "I'ma fuck Ava up."

"Why?" I whined. Reaching over into his lap, and underneath his Nike hoodie, I rubbed my hands up and down his chest. "You didn't miss me today what...were you with Monique?"

He pushed my hands away. "Yo, chill with that dumb shit."

"Whatever. She's disrespected me every time I've seen her. She loves your ass. I know why, though." I smiled, rolling my window down. "It's hot."

Kai sighed, speeding through the streets.

"I know why she loves you." I covered my mouth as a hiccup escaped. "Because the dick is soooo good." I reached into his lap grabbing his dick.

"You drunk, Ma. Sit back and shut up."

Fifteen minutes later, he was pulling into a parking garage. Unbuckling my stilettos, I slipped them off, right along with my jeans, and climbed into his lap.

"Yo, Ma, come on, man." He sighed, helping me adjust in his lap. "You wildin' right now."

I could feel the G-wagon come to a stop.

"Fuck me, Kai," I begged, kissing and sucking on his neck. My tongue traced his tattoos.

Rubbing his hands up and down my back, his warm tongue finally connected with mine. "Mmm ..." I moaned into his mouth. "Make me cum, Kai." I unbuckled his jeans.

Chapter Seventeen

I think I love you

Kai

Blaze was on some real drunk, freaky shit. I'd just pulled into my parking space in the garage of my condo, and she was sitting on my lap, biting on my neck and pulling on my jeans. A nigga aint even gon' front, though. She had my dick hard as fuck. As she pulled my dick out, I unsnapped the buttons on the crotch area of the bodysuit she was wearing. Lifting her up, I slid her down gently.

"Mmm..." she moaned, biting down on my bottom lip. "Right there, baby."

I let my seat back to give us more room. Blaze took that opportunity to plant both of her feet on each side of me. Bouncing up and down on me slowly, she gripped the headrest.

"Fuck..." I groaned, ripping the breast area of her bodysuit to expose her perfect titties. The nipple rings did something to me. Shit was sexy as fuck. I sucked on her left breast and then made my way up to her sweet neck.

"Ooooh." She shivered. "Baby...make me cum," she whined.

I smirked, gripping her hips, moving mine in an upward thrust.

"Oh my God!" She grabbed my face, kissing me.

"Damn, Ma, this pussy wet as fuck," I whispered into her mouth. "Fuck..."

"I'm cumming, baby!" she cried out. As soon as those words left her pretty lips, I felt her wetness soaking my dick and balls.

"Aaaaagh!" She collapsed into my chest. "Shit."

"You wild." I licked my lips helping her back into the passenger seat. "Put your pants back on," I ordered, opening my door. Fixing my jeans, I shut the door.

"You ripped my shirt." She pouted.

"I know." I walked over to her side pulling my hoodie over my head. "Put this on." Handing her the hoodie, I watched as she sluggishly put it on.

"I feel sick, Kai." She looked up at me.

"I'm sure you do, party animal." I shook my head picking her up honeymoon style.

***

"Here. Drink this."

"Ew!" She looked into the glass, frowning. "This is pickle juice."

"I know what it is. Drink it." Pulling my shirt over my head, I sat on the edge of my bed and watched her.

"I don't like pickles."

"Well, you love 'em tonight."

Rolling her eyes, she sipped from the glass. My dick started growing again. Only because Blaze was in my bed, butt-ass naked. Makeup still intact. Hair still pulled up neatly. My baby looked beautiful.

"Why are you looking at me like that?"

"Because I'm a lucky man." She blushed. "Where's all the shit I bought you today?"

When I got home an hour ago, I expected to see shopping bags galore. I knew she'd spent some money. *A lot* of money. Every time she swiped my black card, I got a text notification. Seventeen hundred dollars on Giuseppe heels and shit. She and Ava had a ball on my dime.

"At Ava's. She said she'll drop them off tomorrow," she said placing the empty glass on my nightstand.

166

"A'ight."

She burped, cupping her mouth. "Excuse me."

I laughed. "Yo, I don't like you this drunk."

She grinned. "Why not?"

"Because you too vulnerable."

"Meaning?"

Meaning I got beef with niggas. And I don't want you out drunk partying without me. I told Ava's hardheaded ass that."

"Mehkai really? We were just having fun." She rolled her eyes.

"Didn't I tell you I didn't want you going to no clubs without me?"

She sighed.

"Your ass is hardheaded too."

"You're mean."

"And you're—" My phone went off.

"Who is that calling you this late?" Blaze snatched it up. "Who is Nikki?"

"Nobody." I eyed her.

"Then why the fuck is she calling you at four in the morning?" She scooted off the bed.

"I don't know." I shrugged, stepping out of my jeans.

"Well, let's find out," she slurred answering my phone. "Hello..." She fumbled a little bit with the phone before she put it on speaker. "Hello."

"Who is this?" Nikki smacked her lips.

"I'm Blaze, Kai's wife. Who the fuck is this?"

I shook my head, heading to the master bathroom. Blaze followed me.

"Put Kai on the phone!" Nikki blasted.

"Bitch, don't call this phone after midnight." Blaze hung up as I started the shower.

Her arms were folded across her chest when I turned to face her. Her attempt at mugging me only made me want her little ass even more. "What you poutin' for now?"

"Who is Nikki?" Blaze's look became soft.

Ah shit. These drunk emotions had her bipolar as fuck. Blaze didn't know if she wanted to fuck or fight.

"Is that who you've been with all day?"

"I told you where I been all day." I sighed, stepping in the shower. Hot water from the three shower heads I'd had installed, cascaded down my body.

Blaze stood there looking at me. "Who is she?!"

"Nobody!" I turned my back to her.

"Have you fucked her before?"

I faced her gain. "Why does that matter, Blaze? Get in the shower so we can go to bed. I told you I been handling shit all day. I'm tired."

Defiantly, she crossed her arms over her chest. "Did. You. Fuck. Her?" She paused after each word like I was some kind of dummy.

"Today?" I smirked and her little ass tried to charge at me.

Grabbing her arms, I swiftly turned her around and pushed her into the marble walls. Water ran down our heads as I pressed my body against hers and lifted her arms above her head. Her makeup was running, but it was cool with me. Shit, she looked better without it.

"Get off me," she whined.

"Don't ever try to put your hands on me again." I stared down at her.

"Let me go, Mehkai."

I kissed her hard in the mouth before I did. I watched as she let the water soak her face so she could rub her makeup off. "I'm going back home tomorrow." She huffed. Face now bare. Making her even sexier.

"I doubt that."

"Yeah…we'll see." She reached for the soap, and I pushed her against the glass.

"Mooove."

"Nah." I stood behind her kissing on the back of her neck. "Where you going? Huh?" I bit down on her earlobe sliding into her gushy center.

"Ssss…" she hissed.

"Where the fuck you think you going?" I kept my movements slow, steady, and passionate.

"Oooh, baby," she moaned, putting her forehead on the glass. "I love your dick," she confessed.

"I know you do. Daddy love's this pussy." I bit down on my bottom lip, watching her phat ass slap against my stomach. Unraveling the bun in her hair, I gripped her ponytail, and pulled her head back. Sucking roughly on her neck, I picked my pace up, slamming her down hard on my dick.

"Uuugh!…fuck, shit…ssshit!" she screamed with each thrust.

"Where you going, Blaze?" I asked sucking on the front of her neck.

"No…nowhere baby. I'm not going nowhere." She came and I kept pounding her.

"Tell me you trust me."

"I...baby, Kai..." she whimpered.

"Nah, tell daddy you trust him." I bit down hard on her neck.

"I trust you, Daddy!" she hollered, cumming again.

"I don't want nobody else but you, Ma. I promise," I groaned into her ear before sucking on her earlobe.

"You promise?" She whimpered some more. Pain *and* pleasure plastered on her pretty face.

"Yeah, baby, I promise."

"Oooo...okay, baby," she surrendered.

"Don't nobody matter but you, Blaze." I could feel my nut rising. "You all I give a fuck about." *Shit.*

"Kai..." her legs started shaking. "I'm 'bout to cum again, baby. Wait!"

I locked down on my hold on her. "You gone cum wit' me, Ma?" I groaned loudly into her soft lips. *Fuck.*

"Yeeeessss..."

I blasted in her, holding her little ass up as she came.

"Baaaaaby!" she screamed.

"Fuuuuck," I mumbled underneath my breath. Nah, Blaze wasn't going nowhere. Ever.

Blaze snuggled closer to me, and I kissed her forehead.

"Ma."

"Huh?" she grumbled.

"On some G shit, I need you to trust me." I waited for her response. When she didn't give me one, I lifted her chin for her to look at me.

"Kai, you got females calling you and trying to fight me. I don't want to feel like I have to compete for my man."

"You don't have to compete. Ain't no competition. It's just you. I can't control who calls my phone and when they do."

"Then you need to block their asses," she snapped in hushed tone.

"Done." When the room sat silent for a while, I thought she was sleep.

"Kai."

"Yeah."

"I think I love you."

"Why you think that?"

"I don't know." She sighed into the darkness. "Maybe it's the way you look at me. The way you listen to my problems...and make them *your* problems. Then you fix them." She paused. "It might be the way you make me laugh. You make me feel safe. Like I can depend on you for anything."

"'Cause you can."

She wrapped her arm around me tighter. "It could be the way you spoil me. With affection...and gifts. You're so open with the way you feel about me." She chuckled. "Hell, it's a good chance it might be your sex game. I don't know...but I think I love you."

"Ah yeah?" I kissed her forehead again.

"Yeah," she whispered. "I hope that doesn't confuse any—"

"I think I love you too...probably more."

Chapter Eighteen

Unrequited love

Kenya

"What are you doing here?" I frowned, blocking the entrance to my home. Dressed in nothing but an oversized T-shirt, I crossed my arms across my chest, adjusting my glasses on my nose with my right hand.

"It's snowing. You gone let me in or what?"

"Why should I?"

"'Cause you love me too much to let me freeze to death. You'd be the main one at the funeral bawling and shit." Cole looked down at me with that stupid smirk on his face.

"Don't count on it," I snapped and he pushed his way in.

"Shut up." He closed the door and locked it. "Why is it dark in here?"

"Because it's seven in the morning and I was sleep. What do you want?" Even though I was mad at him, I couldn't deny how sexy Cole was. His locs were pulled up into a neat bun and his lining was on point. His plump lips looked sexy in between his perfectly trimmed mustache and beard.

He walked past me heading up stairs. "Cole..."

"Yo, Kenya, bring your ass on. I'm tired as fuck," he spat over his shoulder. *Still* climbing my stairs.

Asshole. I followed, dragging my feet.

***

I stood leaning against my bedroom threshold eyeing Cole as he removed his clothes.

God, why is this man so perfect?

"Are you getting in the bed or are you just going to stand there grilling me and shit?"

"I can't stand you."

"I know that. Bring your mean ass here." He leaned forward on his legs with his elbows. When I didn't move, he sighed. "Yo, Kenya, come here, Ma. Let me rap wit' you real quick."

Still I didn't budge. If Cole thought he was just going to come here and fuck me, then he was sadly mistaken. His best bet was to hop back on a plane to New York and lay up with one of the *many* bitches he had. Leave me alone. Me *and* my baby. I absentmindedly rubbed my stomach.

"Aye..." He stood up. In nothing but his Polo briefs he swaggered over to me. "What you crying for?"

I hadn't even realized I was. He stood over me, wiping my cheeks with his thumbs.

I sniffled.

"Why are you crying, Kenya? I just came to talk to you. That's all. I didn't come to fuck on you, Ma," he assured me. Kissing my lips softly, he rested his forehead on top of mine. "I missed you."

My heart started pounding. I wondered if he could hear it. *I missed you too.*

"I'm sorry, Ma. Why won't you forgive me?" he asked barely above a whisper. Forehead still on mine.

"Because, Cole, I don't want to just be your baby mama or your fuck buddy." My pride wouldn't allow me to settle even though I loved the hell out of him.

"What do you want from me, Kenya?"

"I want you to only want me Cole."

"Man, Kenya, I *do* only want you. I don't fuck with them bitches like that. Besides Tati, you the only person's feelings I give a fuck about."

I wanted to believe him. Hell, the naïve me did. But I was smarter than that. Cole allowing another woman to scratch him up didn't sit right with me. He wouldn't even let me suck on his neck. Didn't want me leaving hickeys on him.

"What do I have to do to prove you're priority, Kenya? Shit, you carrying my shorty." He rubbed my stomach.

"I don't know." His touch was alluring.

"I want this baby with you, Ma. Just 'cause you mad at me don't mean you take it out on my seed."

As pissed as I was at Cole, I couldn't abort my baby. I wasn't *that* heartless. "I'm keeping the baby, Cole."

He sighed. "Thank you." He pulled me toward my bed, sat down, and pulled me into his lap.

We sat quietly. I couldn't make Cole love me. It had to come natural. He had to *want* to love me. Do right by me. That's probably what hurt the most. Because I knew he wasn't ready.

Cole

Kenya sat in my lap, sniffling. I hated to see her cry, especially because of me. Here she was pregnant with my baby crying over some bullshit. I wouldn't have even fucked Remi had I known the outcome would be this. The shit wasn't even worth it.

"Kenya, stop crying. You're upsetting my shorty. Chill, man." I kissed her face.

"Cole, this is hard for me. I just ended a relationship only to fall in love with a man who ain't ready to love. It's not fair." She continued crying.

"Kenya, man, you know I care about you."

"But?"

"Ain't no *but*. Why are trying to make it seem like I don't. Crying and shit like I ain't been begging for you to hear me out." She was breaking a nigga down. "What? You want me to say I love you? You can't force that love shit on me, shorty."

"You don't think I know that?" She scoffed, hopping out of my lap. "I'm not stupid."

"I didn't say you were." I didn't mind explaining myself to Kenya, but in all honesty, I was getting tired of pleading my case.

"So I'm supposed to wait for you to want to be with me?"

"Is that why you trippin'?" I put my face in hands. "Because you want a relationship? Why you ain't just say that then?"

"Because you're not ready!" she yelled.

"How the fuck you tellin' me what I'm ready for?" Her emotional ass was starting to get on my nerves.

"So you can commit to me and only me?" She stood in front of me. "Nobody else. Just Kenya Danielle Marshall."

"Yeah, I can."

She smacked her lips like she didn't believe me.

"Yo, what the fuck do you want from me?!" I roared, standing up. It was hard for me to ask anybody for forgiveness. I was doing everything except begging on my knees. And the shit still wasn't good enough.

"Don't yell at me!" Her ass started crying again.

"Yo..." This shit was slowly becoming too much. "Kenya, at this point, whatever you wanna do I'm down. If you wanna be with me...okay. If not, that's okay too."

She cried.

"What do you want, Kenya?"

Still she cried.

"Look..." Picking her up, I carried her to her over to the bed and gently laid her down. "Can you stop crying?" Pulling her shirt over her head, I exposed all of her nakedness. *Fuck*. I told her I didn't come here to fuck, but Kenya's body was perfect.

Kissing her lips, I lingered over her, staring into her hazel eyes. Right then and there I knew I had mad love for Kenya. She was everything I needed and wanted in a woman. She was a rider. Kissing on her neck, I sucked down hard on it.

"Cole..." she moaned.

Ignoring her, I kissed down her chest and placed small pecks on her stomach. Opening her legs, I yanked her closer to the edge of the bed. Kissing between her legs, I placed a wet kiss on her pussy. Flicking my tongue up and down her clit, I watched her squirm underneath me.

"Mmm...yes. Right there," she directed.

Lapping up all the juices that dripped from her gushy sex, I sucked on her clit until she tried to run up the bed. Forcefully holding down on her legs, I tongued her pussy down.

"Mmm," I mumbled.

"Yeesss...baby...YES!" She screamed, cumming in my mouth. Shaking. Cursing.

"I love you, Cole...I love you," she whimpered.

Chapter Nineteen

I keep mine

Monique

Standing outside of Mehkai's condo, my hand hovered over the door in a knocking motion. Nervous, that if he opened the door he wouldn't be happy to see me. I'd tried to contact him earlier and I kept getting his voicemail. Finally, deciding I was ready to deal with my fate, I began banging on the door.

"Kai! Open the door. We need to talk!" I kept banging. Heart racing, I waited three minutes before I started banging again.

"Mehkai! I swear on my mother, if you don't—" I stopped yelling when I heard the locks on the door popping. Smirking, I waited to come face to face with him.

"Can I help you?" Blaze opened the door. Frowning. My stomach hurt just looking at her. She was gorgeous.

Dressed in one of Kai's T-shirts, she had her hair pulled up into a crinkly, messy bun. She crossed her arms across her chest, exposing the small cursive tattoo going up the back of her forearm. She tapped her foot on the floor waiting on my response. It was her lips. They had to be what Kai loved the most about her. They were full, pouty, and shiny. I hated her. So much. She smelled like Kai too I noticed, which had me seething.

I hate her.

I clenched my jaws and sighed. "Go get Kai."

"Or what?" she asked calmly, opening the door wider.

"Bitch, just do what I said." I stepped into her personal space. "Or get knocked the fuck out."

I'd done plenty of fighting growing up in the Bronx. All because I was a pretty girl who could dress her ass off. Growing up my mother used to have sex with rich white men, so she kept my closet up to date. We lived smack dead in the middle of the projects, but I stayed wearing designer gear. Bitches couldn't handle me being fine *and* flyy, so whooping ass became something like a hobby. If Blaze wanted to get her ass beat, then that was on her. When she stepped closer to me, she looked up slightly, staring me in the face.

I'm 'bout to fuck this bitch up.

"You ain't knocking shit out," She grilled me. Hard.

Okay, so the bitch had heart. I quickly mushed her dumb ass in the forehead.

183

"Bitch!" She swung at me, hitting me dead in my nose. Immediately, my eyes watered and my vision went black.

I could feel Blaze raining punches on me. Somehow, I managed to grab her by her bun, which to my advantage was loose. Slowly I opened my eyes and yanked her down onto the floor. I was still holding onto her hair when she fell underneath me. I took that opportunity to raise my leg up high and slam my midnight blue Timberland into her face.

"Aaagh!" Blaze yelled, kicking me hard in my stomach, knocking the wind out of me.

"Uuaa." I flew back landing on my ass inside of Kai's condo.

Blaze hopped up charging at me. I tried to get up before she reached me, but she was quicker than I anticipated. I felt my body being knocked back down. The back of my head hit the floor each time I tried to gain leverage.

Fuck! I tried using my feet to turn her over. Knock her down.

Whop

I felt her fist come down on my face.

Whop...whop

An instant pain surged through my left eye and my bottom lip. Blocking my face with my left arm, I swung absentmindedly with my right.

Whop

She hit me in the side of the head and then her foot came down on the side of my face that was exposed.

"Aye!" I heard Kai yell. "What the fuck yo!" He roared snatching a screaming Blaze up. The bitch looked possessed, clawing and punching at him.

"Get the fuck off me!" She tugged away from him, and he threw her over his shoulder. "Let me go!"

"Yo, Blaze!" Kai roared again, making the bones in my body shake.

She hit him in the back as he carried her up the stairs. When I was able to pull myself up off the floor, I took my jacket off and headed after them. If the bitch think she got some shit off, she was dead wrong. She was about to feel me.

I followed the sound of them yelling to Kai's room. He towered over her.

"Chill out! If you hit me again I'ma hit your crazy ass back."

Smack

My eyes widened at the sound of Blaze slapping the shit out of him. His head jerked to the side violently. His shoulders tensed up and he picked her up like she was a rag doll. Throwing her hard, she landed on the middle of the bed.

Racing into the room, I pushed him hard in his back. He faced me scowling, and right then and there I wished I'd just left. I'd never seen Kai look so evil. His eyes were dark, forehead crinkled, and his eyes furrowed. Even his breathing was off. I could tell from the way his bare chest heaved up and down. He looked like the murderer everyone in New York gossiped about.

"Get out." He eyed me.

"Kai—"

"Mo, get the fuck out!" He pushed me back.

Blaze scooted off the bed.

"Yo, Blaze, get back on the bed," he warned her, still looking down at me.

"So it's her over me?" I asked appalled. I couldn't even hold back my tears. "It's like that?" My chest burned. Kai was breaking my heart.

Blaze rushed in our direction and Kai held her back with his arm. She swung at me and missed by an inch. I swung back, and missed because Kai pushed her backwards. Shoving her onto the bed, he grabbed me by the back of my neck and led me out of the room. He slammed the door in my face and I lost all my sanity.

"Kai! Open the door!" I screamed at the top of my lungs.

I'd never felt so disrespected in my life. Backing away from his door I sighed in defeat. He'd chosen Blaze. I couldn't compete where I didn't compare. Storming out of his condo, I picked my jacket up. If Kai didn't want me, he didn't deserve me. I was done. We were done. Fuck him.

Blaze

"Open the door, Blaze." Mehkai's rough voice demanded.

I sat on the side of the Jacuzzi tub, face in my hands. Pissed...enraged. My lip and right cheek were throbbing from when Monique put her damn Timberland on my face. I didn't have to look in the mirror to know my face was bruised and my lip was busted. I wanted to kill her.

"Blaze!"

I wanted to kill his ass too.

"Ma, open the fuckin' door." His voice blared. The loud thud on the door let me know he'd punched it.

I wasn't fazed one bit. However, I did jump from my seat when the frame of the door cracked and the door flew open.

Kai walked over to me. Staring down at me, he rubbed my cheek. "Yo, you been really buggin' the fuck out lately."

I rolled my eyes. "Whatever."

He lifted my chin. "You a'ight?"

"Do I look all right?"

"Monique gon' get hers, so don't even worry," he assured me, lifting my chin to inspect my lip. "You allergic to anything?"

I frowned. "Cats."

"No medicine?"

"No."

Letting me go, he opened the medicine cabinet above the sink.

"Kai, I'm not fighting over you again." He picked me up and sat me down on the counter, "Did you hear me?"

Pouring two pills in his palm he tried handing them to me. I eyed him, shaking my head no. Sighing, he sat them down on the counter next to me.

"Kai..."

"I heard you, Blaze. I told you I would handle it, didn't I?"

I looked at him. His left cheek was red from where I'd slapped him and he had scratches on his shoulders from where I'd clawed at him. Guilt washed over me. It wasn't his fault a fight between Monique and I had broken out. On more than one occasion, he'd let it be known she didn't mean anything to him. It was *her* who had a hard time letting go.

"I'm sorry," I huffed.

"You straight." He pressed a cold towel on my cheek.

Chapter Twenty

... Forgive me?

Kenya

"She what?!" I yelled into the phone. Cole looked over at me. "Oh hell no!"

"Yeah, kicked me in my face and everything." Blaze scoffed.

"Ok, I'ma see if I can get a plane ticket. Let me call you back."

"Ken, no. I'm cool. I whooped her ass."

"Where the fuck was Kai?"

"In the shower."

"See. I'ma whoop his ass too!"

"I already did." She sighed.

Good girl. "He didn't hit you back did he?" I wasn't scared of Kai, Cole, or nobody in their little crew. They could all feel my wrath behind Blaze.

"No. He was pissed, though. Still is. He hasn't been really talking to me."

"You sure I don't need me to come to New York?" I stood up, making my way to my closet. "Fuck that I'm about to book a flight." I was livid.

"Aye..." Cole stood behind me. "Yo ass aint going nowhere. Go lay back down."

"Hold on, Blaze." I rolled my eyes. "This don't have nothing to do with you."

He frowned. Snatched the phone out of my hand. "Yo, Blaze, put Kai Money on the phone," he ordered, walking back out of my closet.

I followed. Hands on my hips. "Give me my phone back."

"Yo, what up, Kai? Whatever Blaze's criminal-minded ass is planning out there, tell her to keep my shorty out of it."

Snitch

"Yeah...aight." He sat down on the bed handing me my phone.

Snatching it out of his hand, I placed it back to my ear. "Blaze?"

"Yeah, I' m here. Tell Cole snitches get stitches." She chuckled.

"No, they get put in ditches. He should know." I mugged him.

"I'm cool though, Ken. I'm leaving tomorrow night."

"'Cause of her?"

"No. I have some work to do that I bailed out on to be here."

"Ok. Well, hurry up and come home. I miss you. I had to have breakfast with Amina."

She giggled. "She still hate me?"

"You know it." I smiled.

"What did you have to tell me anyways?"

"I'll tell you when you get back. I want to say it face to face." I rubbed my flat stomach and plopped down on Cole's lap.

"You sure? I'm not in a rush to get off the phone," she whined quietly. "Kai's being mean." I knew she was pouting.

"You whooped his ass. I would be mad at you too." I laughed. She was just tellin' me I shouldn't put my hands on Cole. Hypocrite.

"Mind your business." Cole shook his head turning on the PlayStation 4 he claimed he'd bought for me last month. The only game I had was 2K, so I knew better.

"Blaze is my business." I put the phone on speaker. "Ain't that right, Blaze?"

"Yep."

"You should go to the Statue of Liberty before you go." I knew how bad Blaze wanted to see it in person.

"He won't even sit in the same room as me. He said we were cool, but he's been standoffish."

"Go suck his dick and make him a sandwich." I grinned. I'm sure Blaze was red in the face.

"Kenya! Can Cole hear you?"

"Yep," he answered picking his team. Mocking her.

"You're so embarrassing. You get on my nerves!" she went off.

"Don't worry, Giggles." He chose the Knicks. "She only half done. Go make me a sandwich." He slapped my thigh.

Blaze laughed. "Ew."

Cutting my eyes at Cole, I stood up. "I'll call you back, B. Let me know if you change your mind."

"I won't. I'll call you tomorrow."

"Ok. Later, chica."

Kai

I was sitting in one of the spare bedrooms I'd made my office when Blaze knocked on the door. Putting the blunt I'd been hitting down, I sucked my teeth. I wasn't trying to deal with her aggressive ass right now. Blaze lucky I fucks with her the long way. It took everything in me not to choke her when she hit me. Her hits weren't hard enough to cause me any real physical pain, but I'd asked her more than once to keep her hands to herself.

"What?" I asked.

She pushed the door open. "Can I come in?"

"You already let yourself in. What up?" I eyed her standing in nothing but a peach lace panty and bra set.

"What are you doing?" she asked innocently, stepping further into the room.

Lifting one of the thick stacks of cash in my hands, I nodded my head. "Counting up. What's wrong?"

"Nothing. I was about to cook. You have any recommendations?"

Beautiful. How perfect she was, was all I could focus on as she bit down on her bottom lip. Whatever she sprayed on after she got out the shower was polluting the air around me; some fruity shit, Ava had dropped off with all her shopping bags. Her hair was damp, hanging in loose curls surrounding her face. Even though she was on my shit list, Blaze had my dick hard.

"Come here." I placed the stack I was holding down on my desk and pushed my chair back a little. She obliged, walking towards me, still biting on that bottom lip. When she reached me, I picked her up by the bottom of her ass and sat her down on my desk directly in front of me.

She tucked her hair behind her ears; avoiding eye contact.

"Your lip hurt?" It wasn't busted, just puffy.

She shook her head no.

"Cheek still sore?" I noticed the swelling was going down.

Again, she just shook her head. We stared at each other when she finally grew the courage to look me in the eyes. I meant what I said when I told her I would handle Monique. Mo wanted to learn the hard way, and I was about to teach her ignorant ass not to fuck wit' mines. Blaze...was mine. And it was my sole purpose to protect and provide for her. Even though I'd witnessed her beating Mo's ass, she still had another one coming. Soon.

"Are you hungry?" she asked in a low tone.

"Yeah."

"What do you want to eat?"

"It's some chicken in there. Whatever you can come up with, I'm down." I shrugged.

"Okay." She sighed. Sliding off of my desk, she surprised me when she dropped to her knees in front of me.

Blaze hadn't sucked my dick yet, I assumed she'd do it when she felt comfortable. I leaned back in my chair, lifting up in my seat a little to pull my briefs and sweats down. I looked down at Blaze in awe. My baby. The best thing that's happened in my life, making my fucked up reality a lot more tolerable. She wrapped her soft lips around the head of my dick, running her tongue along the tip. Her hands massaged the length of my dick as she came down my shaft.

"Mmm." I murmured. Couldn't take my eyes off of her. Even when I could feel the back of her throat and I felt my eyes get real heavy.

Fuck

She came back up slowly, spitting on my dick. "Mmm …" She moaned….Head bobbing up and down slowly in my lap.

Shit

I bit down on my lip. Fighting to stay in control of the situation. Of the nut I felt myself succumbing to. *Fuck*. Blaze wasn't playing fair.

Her bobbing sped up and my toes curled over. She grabbed my balls into her slimy hands massaging them. "Mmm," she groaned. Like my dick was a lollipop...her favorite flavor.

Fuck it. I grabbed the top of her head and threw my head back.

"Yeah...suck this muthafucka," I growled.

"Mmmmmm."

"You want Daddy to cum in yo' mouth?" I bit down on the corner of my lip. Blaze had me sweating fucking bullets.

Coming up a little, she licked the tip of my dick, "Cum in my mouth, baby," she purred.

My eyes shot open. I had to see it. I had to see Blaze swallowing my babies. She quickened her pace; head bobbing, spit trickling down my nuts, jacking me off with both hands. The euphoria growing from my toes, up my legs, and through my torso was a lot on a nigga.

I felt the vein in my neck expand and it was a wrap. "Fuuuuck." My dick jerked as I blasted down her throat. My baby took it all like a champ.

"Mmm." She sucked on the head of my dick making sure she got every last drop. Looking up at me with heavy bedroom eyes. She stood up to her feet as I attempted to catch my breath. Wiping her mouth, Blaze smiled.

"I'll come get you when dinner is ready." She leaned forward and kissed my forehead.

Pulling my briefs and sweats back up, I watched her switch out. Yeah, my baby was the shit.

Chapter Twenty-One

Rock-a-bye baby

Kenya

"Why'd you pick here?" Blaze sat down across from me. "When you said meet up for lunch, I thought you meant for food," she pouted looking around.

"I like frozen yogurt. Plus..." I shrugged. "Cole made me a big breakfast before work so I'm full."

She frowned. Rolled her eyes. "You should've said that. I would've stopped at Buffalo Wild Wings."

"My fault."

"So are you and Cole an item now?" She smiled, leaning forward on the table.

"We've *been* an item," I corrected her forgetful ass. She rolled her eyes at me.

"You know what I mean. Is it official?" Blaze anticipated my answer.

I cheesed, nodding my head up and down. "Yep. We's married now." I gave my best rendition of a Southern bell.

Blaze cracked up laughing. "You get on my nerves."

I laughed with her. "He's stuck with me for life now. Ain't no breaking up, bitch." And even though I was tittering, I was dead serious. Blaze didn't know the half of it.

"Your ass is crazy." She shook her head. "But I'm happy for you guys. I still need to have a conversation with Cole."

I cut my eyes at her.

"You can make that face all you want." She was unbothered.

"Let it go. I did."

She shrugged. "I'll think about it."

"Didn't you just beat up Kai?" I asked with a raised eyebrow.

"Touché." She nodded. Standing up, she headed for the counter.

I followed suit. "That's not all, B."

"What?" We reached the counter. "What's the matter?" She asked, staring down at the yogurt behind the glass; mentally picking through flavors.

"Well..." She pointed at the kind she wanted. "Blaze, you're going to be a god mommy."

She looked over at me and then down at my stomach. "You lyin'." The corners of her mouth turned upward.

"Nope." I beamed. "We're pregnant." I said *we* as in Blaze too. I knew she would treat my baby like her own.

"Aaagggh!" Blaze yanked me up into her arms. Strong ass.

"Really?" I laughed uncontrollably. "Put me down crazy."

"Kenya! You're going to be a mommy. You're about to have a little you!" she squealed. "Oh my God! I hope it's a girl so you can name her after me."

I shook my head. "I want a boy."

"I'll take one of those too." She shrugged, letting me go, but then draped her arm over my shoulders. "Blaze is unisex."

I rolled my eyes, pushing her off me. "You silly."

"So what did Cole say? Have you told him?"

"Yeah, as soon as I found out. I think that's part of the reason his ass came back down here." Blaze paid for our frozen yogurt. "He's been here for three days now. Getting on my damn nerves." I complained. Fronting like I wasn't ecstatic about being next to him. Sexing him...whenever I wanted.

"Y'all so cute." She giggled.

"That's my booboo," I cooed. "Arrogant ass."

"You love it." She smiled.

"I do. I love him, Blaze." I sighed. "What I'ma do?" I took a bite of yogurt. "Ima end up killing him."

She burst into a fit of laughter. "Okay, killer Kenya. Deranged ass."

"I got him to trade me phones for the day."

Blaze raised an eyebrow.

"Yeah, but he gave it up too freely."

"He might have a second phone." She shrugged. "Kai does."

"And you're okay with that?"

"Hell no." She grimaced. "But I trust Mehkai. So if he tells me I don't have nothing to worry about, then I'm going to take his word."

My best friend was in love. My heart smiled. "You're right, I have to trust him."

"Yep," she encouraged eagerly.

Right on cue, Cole's phone started ringing in my purse. "That's him now." I said retrieving it. I frowned when I saw the contact wasn't saved.

"What's wrong?"

"The number's not saved." I looked to her. "Should I answer it?"

"I don't see why not. It might be important."

I nodded. "You're right." Sliding the clear bar to answer, I placed it to my ear. "Hello?"

"Who is this? Where is Cole?" A woman's voice blared through the phone's speaker. New Jersey accent thick.

"Kenya. Cole's not with me right now. What do you want?" Blaze's eyes were on mine. Probably trying to read me. She was good at that...reading people.

"Hoe. Put my baby father on the phone and quit playing with me. You hoes get a little dick and think shit is sweet. The fuck outta here." She was pissed.

"LaRell...is it?" I knew. "Like I said, my name is Kenya. I'm Cole's woman."

"This desperate bitch." She snorted and another woman in her background laughed. "Put my baby's father on the phone, *Kenya*."

"Like I said. He's not with me, he's at home. Sleep. Tired. From all the fuckin' we been doing." I smirked and Blaze started choking.

"Where you at bitch!" she screeched. "I'm 'bout to pull up."

"You gotta book a flight first."

"Cole gon' have your nappy-ass head when he hears about this. You can guarantee," she informed me as a threat.

"The only head Cole worries about when it comes to me, *LaRell*, is when his face is deep in my pussy. Ooooh...and when his dick is in my mouth." Blaze was laughing. Hard. Egging me on. If Cole was here, he'd be pissed.

"When will you sewer rats learn? Baby mama ain't going nowhere." Her tone of voice let me know she was smirking. "He aint never gon' stop fuckin' me."

"Well, I guess we're sister wives. Tell Tati she might get the little brother she always wanted. Thank me later. In about six months to be exact."

The line went quiet. *Got that ass.*

"You're lying. You ain't pregnant by Cole. He's not that sloppy. He wouldn't do no shit like that."

Oh, so your feelings are hurt.

"Put Cole on the phone now. I'm done playing with you," she warned me.

"I'm not laughing. Now, Cole will call you back when I get home." I started to rush her off the phone.

"Tell Cole, he won't have shit else to do with my daughter."

"Girl," she hung up on me before I could get another word out.

"Who was that?" Blaze gave me a quizzical look from across the table.

"Cole's baby mama." I sighed.

"What did she say?"

"She asked could she speak to Cole and then got indignant when I told her he wasn't with me."

"So why'd you tell her you were pregnant? You should've let Cole handle that."

She was right.

"The bitch's mouth was becoming too reckless. I had to shut her loud ass up," I defended my reasoning.

"Okay. But you need to tell Cole you told her before she does. That's kind of a conversation he should've had with her. Not you." Blaze didn't look pleased with me.

"Oh shut up. Mother hen. She was going to find out eventually. I just sped the process up." I became defensive. Whose side was she on?

"It's your relationship not mine." She threw her hands up in defeat. "I don't have to deal with Cole," she informed me

"Ain't nobody worried about Cole." I waved her off.

"Okay."

"So..." I had to get the heat off of me. "You love Kai Money...huh?" I grinned.

Her face scrunched up in disapproval. "Stop calling him Kai Money."

"Why? It kind of rolls off the tongue." I kept grinning. Fucking with her.

"Because that's not who he is."

I was lost. I'm guessing Blaze saw the confusion on my face so she reiterated. "Kai Money isn't who Mehkai is." She had this faraway look in her eyes. "Mehkai's a man. A *strong* man..." she clarified. I smiled. "With a big heart and a damaged past. *Mehkai* is caring, charismatic, intelligent, and understanding."

Awww Blaze, I cooed inwardly.

"*Kai Money* isn't any of that. Kai Money...he's unapproachable. Cold...broken." Her voice trailed off before she cleared her throat. "I like *Mehkai* better anyway."

"Well...I don't know *Mehkai*, I know Kai Money. Kai. So I'll leave that to you." I finished off my frozen yogurt.

We sat for about thirty minutes chatting about local news, celebrity buzz, work, the baby, and her trip to New York. In that order. I was happy *Mehkai* was bringing Blaze out of her shell. She was different; of course in a good way. She was glowing. Blaze was content.

You go girl.

Chapter Twenty-Two

Put some respect on it

Cole

After making sure shit with Kenya was straight, I was back home in New York. Thanksgiving was coming up, and regardless of me and LaRell's situation, we always spent holidays as a family together for Tati. I didn't grow up in a two-parent home and even though technically, me and Rell wasn't together, I wanted Tati to always have us both there. Pulling up next to a free gas pump, I put my car in park and looked out my review mirror. The gas station was packed as fuck for it to be so late.

Opening my glove compartment, I pulled my burner out and sat it in my lap. My eyes shifted around the parking lot just checkin' out the scenery. What caught my attention was a group of four niggas posted on the hood of two blue muscle cars. They couldn't see me behind my tint, but they were staring in my direction. Rubbing my chin, I kept my gaze locked in on them. Finally, they huddled back up and turned away.

Popping the locks, I opened my door and hopped out. Before I shut the door, I made sure my gun was tucked. Glancing up at the pump number, I took off walking toward the entrance. Just as I reached the door, it swung open and almost hit me in the face.

"The fuck?!" I grilled the little chick coming out.

"My bad." She rolled her eyes.

"Yeah, watch what the fuck you doin' shorty." I held the door open so she could get by.

"Rude ass," she hissed, switching away.

Shaking my head, I walked into the store, hitting the nigga behind the counter with a quick head nod. As I opened the glass freezer door, I heard the bells to the front door chime.

"Fuck you lookin' at, nigga." I looked up to see one of the cats from the parking lot head to the chip aisle.

Dude behind the counter raised his hands in a mock surrender. "I don't want any problems." His eyes shot in my direction.

Grabbing a soda, I headed to the front. "What up, boss? Let me get two Backwoods and forty on six." I placed a fifty on the counter. I could feel dude walk up behind me. Getting my change, I left the store.

Loud music could be heard as I made my way to my car, tossed all my shit in the passenger's seat and popped my gas door open. Shorty that almost hit me with the door approached the back of my truck as I put the nozzle in.

"The fuck you want?" I mugged her.

"Damn." She smiled. "Why you gotta be so rude? I can't come and say hey?"

I glared down at her. Looking over my shoulder, I noticed them niggas had finally hopped in their whips. "Yo, shorty, get the fuck away from my ride." An eerie feeling came over me.

"Destiny." She held her hand out.

I looked at that shit like it was contaminated. "Yo, Ma, are you deaf?" I glanced back over my shoulder again.

"So it's like that?" She smirked. "Gon' straight diss me like that?" Her eyes shot across the parking lot.

Following her gaze, I noticed the back door to one of the muscle cars opened and somebody got out. Clenching my jaw, I coolly took the nozzle out at thirty dollars. Shutting the small door, I turned away from her and the moment I opened my door, gunshots fired.

Quickly jumping in my ride, I shut the door, leaned over in the passenger's seat, and started the truck. Pulling the gears back, I peeled off and sped out of the parking lot. The bullets that were hitting my truck, made it rock just a little as they followed me down the street.

"Fuck!" I hit the steering wheel in rage. "Fuck!" Looking out my rearview as I sped through a red light, and hit the corner, I watched them do the same.

Speeding down the street I hit another corner and shot through a residential neighborhood. Just as I was coming up on a stop sign, two of my tires were blown out and the truck swerved right through it. Trying my best to control my whip, I managed to come to a fucked up stop when my passenger's side smacked against a tree.

"Fuck!" I quickly hopped out the truck running behind a house. Hopping a fence I ended up on the next block just as a bullet whizzed past my head. Somebody was about to die.

I hopped a few more fences before I didn't hear them loud-ass hemi's from their cars. Out of breath, I leaned against a wooden fence. Pulling my phone from my back pocket, I pulled up Nasir.

"Yo." Loud music boomed from his end.

"Ayo, some shit came up, meet me at the spot on Linden." I disconnected the call and took off speed walking.

***

"Nigga, what the fuck happened to you?" Nas and Quan started down the stairs toward me.

I stormed past them and into the trap house. I was hit with the smell of weed when I entered and a few greetings as I made my way to the kitchen.

"Yo, what the fuck is up?" Nas asked this time. Quan followed behind him, eating an apple.

"Got caught slippin' and shit." I reached down into the cabinet underneath the sink.

"Where at?"Quan sat down at the beat-up wooden kitchen table.

"At BP." I removed an AR, making sure it was fully loaded. Sittin' it down on the counter, I checked the time on my phone.

"Shit, let's head back over there." Nas started back for the front door. Quan stood up.

***

"Niggas went back and posted up." Quan chuckled, pulling his ski mask over his head. "They said fuck you, Cole."

Nas laughed and then took a toke from the blunt he was smokin' on. "Gangster shit."

"Fuck y'all. Nas pull up on them niggas." I cocked my gun.

"Hol' up." Quan leaned forward in his seat. "Aint that, that nigga Jamarcus?" He inched his tinted window down.

Sure enough, it was. I watched as he limped over in crutches to the passenger's side of one of the blue cars. He dapped one of the homies up and pulled ole girl that almost smacked me with the door, into a tight hug and kissed her.

"This nigga too comfortable." Quan cocked his gun.

Nas, the only one not wearing a ski mask, pulled up on his side and rolled his window down. "What up, homies?" He smiled, sitting his glock in his lap.

"Fuck you want?" I heard somebody say.

212

Easing my window down, I pulled the trigger back and started lighting shit up. They didn't even have time to shoot back when Nas started letting rounds off too. Screams and hollers could be heard not only from the people at their cars, but from the few people who were just in the parking lot trying to get gas. The chick went down, and Jamarcus pushed her off of him. Quan opened his door, got out, and rushed him.

"Aye, I'm not from here!" Jamarcus cowered in fear.

Scooting across the seat, I got out and took my burner out from behind me. His eyes widened in terror when I pulled my ski mask up over my eyes and sneered down at him. "Kai can't save you now." Pressing on the trigger twice, I shot him in the head.

"Yo, Quan run in there and get them surveillance tapes." I made my way back to Nas' whip. Before I could shut the door, he was already driving to the front of the convenience store.

"I shoulda told that nigga to get me a honeybun." He leaned back in his seat. "I got the munchies like a muthafucka."

No more than one minute later, Quan ran out of the store carrying two tapes and a bag of Doritos. Hopping in the passenger's seat, he slammed the door shut. Nas sped out of the parking lot and drove in the opposite way from where we had arrived.

"We straight." Quan pulled his ski mask off.

"A'lght." I leaned back in my seat.

"Yo, Cole..." Nas looked back at me from the rearview mirror. "What you gon' tell that nigga. Kai Money? Ain't that family or some shit?"

"I ain't tellin' Kai shit." I smirked. "That lil nigga was hangin' wit' the wrong niggas and fell victim to the streets." I checked the time on my phone.

"You wild." Nas laughed.

Fuck Jamarcus. He wasn't no kin to me.

Chapter Twenty-Three

Daddy, meet...the man of my dreams

Blaze

"You ready?" I looked over at Mehkai.

"Do I have a choice?" He gave me a quick one-sided smile.

"Not at all, my friend." I smiled back.

Turning the car off, he licked his lips and rubbed his hand across the shiny waves on his head.

"How do I look?" I pulled the sun visor down.

"Beautiful." Opening his door he got out.

I cheesed. Mehkai complimented me all the time. I could be walking past him, giving my opinion on something, or just laying across his lap reading a book. He always made me feel wanted...sexy. I laughed in my head when I remembered him sitting in the bathroom with me while I did my hair.

I was standing in front of my bathroom mirror when he swaggered in, put the lid down, and sat on the fluffy grey cushion. He glanced up at me as I looked down in wonderment at him. Didn't say a word to me as he looked down at his

phone; returning texts, deleting messages. I figured he was
trying to rush me because he was fully dressed and I was still
in my underwear. Out of nowhere, he grabbed a handful of my
behind and shook it lightly.

My thoughts were broken when my door was pulled open and Mehkai helped me out.

"You a'ight?" He shut my door.

"Yeah..." The front door to my dad's ranch-styled home opened, and he stepped outside.

"Took you long enough!" He crossed his arms across his chest.

"Happy Thanksgiving to you too, Papa." I rolled my eyes as Mehkai followed me up the walkway.

"Happy Thanksgiving," he offered a smile, stepping to the side to let us in. "Happy Thanksgiving, young man." He nodded to Mehkai, closing the door.

"Same to you."

We followed my dad into the dining room, where his sister, Evelyn, and her daughter, my favorite cousin, Eve, were sitting. I smiled upon seeing their faces, letting go of Mehkai's hand.

"Auntie!" I squealed, rushing to her side. Bending down to give her a hug and planting a juicy kiss on her fluffy cheek.

"Hey, Nina Bonita!" She melted. "How have you been?" She looked from me to Mehkai and then back to me again.

"I've been okay." I nudged Eve. "Hey, big head."

Smiling, she pinched me playfully. "I've been calling you. Don't try to speak to me now."

I leaned down behind her, wrapped my arm around her shoulders and pulled her into a tight embrace. "Don't be like that, Pookie." I kissed the side of her face.

"Ew don't put your lips on me." She tittered. "I don't know where they've been." I pecked her again. I loved my Eve.

"I can take a guess." Evelyn's thick Spanish accent was laced with conviction.

Mehkai chuckled.

Rising up, I shook my head. Embarrassed. Auntie Evelyn had no filter.

"Aren't you going to introduce us to your friend?" Her eyes danced around Mehkai.

"Oh yeah." I went to stand by my baby. "That was rude of me." I grabbed his hand. "Papa, this is Mehkai, my boyfriend."

My dad nodded his head, taking Mehkai in.

"Baby, this is my dad, Sebastian, my auntie, Evelyn, and my little cousin, Eve."

"Nice to meet you." Mehkai nodded.

"I'm not little, Blaze." Eve frowned. "I'll be twenty-one in thirteen weeks," she corrected me.

"Until then, your ass is little," Evelyn chimed in.

"Whatever," Eve mumbled, rolling her eyes. Aunt Evelyn didn't see it , though. Eve knew better.

"Nice to meet you too, honey." She stood to her feet and extended her hand. Mehkai gave her a gentle handshake.

"We've crossed paths before." My dad said as he and Mehkai did some kind of fist handshake. Probably a man thing. "Next time you drag my daughter out of a room, make sure she comes back smiling."

Mehkai gave that one-sided smile again. "I got you."

There was a knock at the front door.

"That's probably Viola and them." Evelyn stood to answer.

"I got it." I reassured her, looking to Kai to make sure he felt comfortable. It almost went unnoticed, but he nodded. Leaving the dining room, I could hear Eve talking to Mehkai.

"Doesn't teardrops on your face mean you've killed a guy?"

Lord

Kai

"What kind of question is that to ask a person?" Blaze's fathers scoffed at Eve.

She shrugged, reaching for her phone. "I'm just saying."

"Mehkai, have a seat." Her aunt Evelyn pointed to an empty chair.

"Nah, we men are about to go have a few drinks while you wonderful ladies set the table." Sebastian winked at her.

"Family!"

"Hey, blacky." Evelyn cheesed standing up to greet an older black man.

"What's going on taco breath?" He grinned pulling her into a tight embrace.

"Hey, Uncle Monty." Eve looked up from her phone.

"Hey, pumpkin face." He winked at her.

"I thought I was pumpkin face." I heard Blaze. She rounded the corner with two chicks between her and Eve's age. A baby on her hip. A smile on her pretty face.

"We all are." The first chick sat down at the table. She was thick as fuck, with pretty milk chocolate skin covered in tattoos.

"Right," the second joined her. "Sup, Unc? Hey Auntie Ev. Hey, Eve." She waved across the table.

"Y'all all my pumpkin faces," he confirmed.

Sebastian chuckled.

I looked around the room, playing the background when another woman entered. Same soft skin tone as the two dark skin beauties sitting at the table.

"Why don't I smell food?" She walked past Blaze, pinching her on the cheek, smiling.

"Because your ass is always late, Viola." Sebastian expressed. "Where's the damn turkey?"

"In the car. Toya, go get it." She tapped the second chick on the shoulder.

"Why me?" she asked appalled. "Have Nisha go."

"Because I said." Viola ice grilled her little ass. "Get your ass up and go."

Monty let out a hearty laugh. "Leave my baby alone." He rubbed the top of Toya's head as she stomped past him.

"That's her problem now. Her ass is spoiled. All of 'em. Nisha, Eve, and Blaze too." She gave Evelyn a side hug and they exchanged quick squeezes.

"Who do we have here?" Her eyes finally landed on mine.

"Kai." I extended my hand.

"Well, hello, Kai. You're an awfully handsome young man," she complimented me.

"Isn't he?" Evelyn cosigned. "Blaze, you did well." Viola cheesed up at me.

"Auntie..." Blaze cut her eyes. I smiled. My baby was jealous.

"Welcome to the family." Viola gave me a motherly hug.

***

"Mehkai, you drink?" Sebastian asked. We were now sitting in his den. I watched as he poured up Jack Daniels in five double shot glasses.

"Yeah..."

"Bastian, I can't believe you letting Blaze have a boyfriend." Monty lit a cigar.

I glowered at him, offended. Daddy or not, aint no nigga *letting* me do shit. I'm a grown-ass man. Blaze was mine because there was no other woman that could compare. And I was hers for that same reason. I'm sure Monty was only joking, but I wasn't feeling that. Me and Blaze were meant to be. Fuck consent.

"My baby girl is growing up. She's smart, beautiful, and independent. I'm proud of her," Sebastian boasted.

"Me too. Thank God Eve and Toya are following in her footsteps. Nisha's ass is the one I don't understand," Monty stressed. "You know she's stripping now?" He took a shot.

"Yeah...mi amor told me." I assumed he was referring to Blaze.

"She's older than all of them. She knows better than that shit," Monty spat. Disappointed.

"Give her time, man. You know how women are. Confused as hell." Sebastian took two shots back to back.

Lord, don't give me a daughter.

"Tell me about it. Viola's been getting on my damn nerves."

Sebastian laughed then looked at me. "You got any kids, Mehkai?"

"Nah."

"Good." Monty scoffed. "Don't have any."

"Don't have any what?" Eve entered the den holding three Coronas. "Ma told me to bring these down here." She sat them down on the table. "Can I have a drink?"

"Hell no!" Sebastian glared at her.

Monty shook his head. "Evelyn would kill us and serve *us* for dinner." He reached for his Corona. "Crazy ass Latina."

"I'm practically grown."

"And I'm practically telling you to get your grown ass on," Sebastian checked her. She spun on her heels, stomping the entire way out of the den.

"See what I mean?" Monty pointed toward the door. "They grow up too damn fast."

I shrugged.

"So how long have you and my daughter been an item?" Sebastian leaned back in his seat.

"For a minute. That's my baby." I popped open my Corona.

"And you don't live here?"

"Nah."

"New York, she said. How is it?" He took a drink.

"It's cool." I wasn't one for being questioned by anyone. I hated it. Made me feel like I was being interrogated and shit.

"What do you do for a living?" Was his next question. And I knew it would be. "Blaze says her rent is paid up for a year." The way he looked at me let me know he assumed I had something to do with that. And I did. "Said her car is completely paid off." I'd done that too, he knew.

"I have a few businesses out in New York and in Jersey."

"Oh yeah?" Monty finished off his drink. "What kind?"

I now had two set of eyes on me. Filling me out. I couldn't be mad, though. They loved Blaze. Probably as much as I did or close. They were just protecting her. I could respect that.

"A few auto shops, I dabble in real estate, got two bars out on the Jersey shore." I took the rest if my drink down. That was it. That's all they were getting out of me. I hadn't lied, though.

"Good job, young man." Monty gave me a nod of approval. "Good to see young black men making shit happen."

"Respect." I nodded in his direction.

Sebastian continued giving me the side eye. I didn't give two fucks. I hoped the look I gave him back let that be known. The less he knew about me, the better.

"Papa..." Blaze poked her head into the room, reminding who I was even doing this corny shit for.

"Mi amor?"

"We're setting the table up now. Go wash up." Her eyes darted to mine. "You okay?"

"I'm straight." I stood, walking toward her.

"You sure?" She tried to read my body language. That lip poked out and she shot her eyes in her father's direction.

"Yeah, Ma, I'm good." I kissed her forehead and chuckled at her readiness to defend me. Blaze was choosing, and I was blessed to have been picked.

Chapter Twenty-Four

Look who's coming to dinner

Blaze

Sitting next to Mehkai, I listened to my aunts talking about when they were my cousins' and my age. My Aunt Viola high-fived my Aunt Evelyn every three minutes, reminiscing. Uncle Monty kept calling them whores, my dad was agreeing, and my cousins and I were cracking up. They had us holding our stomachs, wiping our eyes, holding onto each other. Mehkai even chuckled a little.

"Viola, quit lying!" Uncle Monty shook his head. "You tried to poison me."

I giggled, bouncing my little cousin, Rome, in my lap. We finally had a boy, thanks to Aunt Viola and Uncle Monty's freaky asses. They were almost fifty with a nine month old. They bickered all the time, but they were riding for each other till the wheels fell off. I loved their relationship.

"I told you to stay away from her didn't I?" Her perfectly arched brow rose.

"So you were going to kill them, Ma?" Toya asked in disbelief.

"I sure in the hell was." Her and Aunt Evelyn slapped fives again. "Ev and Frankee helped me make it." They laughed some more.

"Auntie Frankee didn't play." Nisha sipped from her cup.

"Right," Toya cosigned of course.

The mention of my mother's name made me feel uneasy. Why would they bring her up? It was like some unspoken rule not to bring her up, at least not around me. She'd abandoned me. Us. Our family. And for what? To be with Uncle Monty's brother, my dad's best friend.

She'd turned her back on this family when she and Jarvis skipped town. Broke my father's heart. Thanksgiving was about being thankful and grateful for all the things you had. People you knew loved you. Hence the reason *she* wasn't here. *Hadn't* been here in fourteen years.

I looked around at the mother-daughter duos in the room and a new emotion for Frankee formed. Hate. She'd left me to have a whole new set of kids. She started a new life. Making it quite clear she didn't want me a part of it. Her daughter.

227

I scoffed.

"You aight?" Mehkai whispered in my ear.

Had he noticed my sudden gloomy disposition? I'd gotten so lost in my thoughts about Frankee, I prayed I wasn't mugging, or worse...tearing up. I couldn't break down here. In front of them over *her.*

"Yeah, I'm fine. Just full and sleepy." He leaned back into his seat, arm still draped across the couch behind me.

I needed some air. Passing Rome to Nisha, I pushed up from the sofa. "You okay, amor?" My dad looked at me with steady eyes.

"Yeah, it's getting hot so I'm going to stand outside." *Far away from y'all, since y'all like to bring up irrelevant people.* I frowned, now mad at everybody in the room. I felt betrayed.

Mehkai followed close behind me as I hauled ass to the exit. I needed to get away before I snapped. I snagged my coat off the closet by the door. Once we stepped outside, I welcomed the chilly, late November air. Snow from last week's snow storm graced the icy pavement. Zipping my coat up, I placed my hands in the pockets. My nose was the first to freeze over.

"What's wrong?" Mehkai stood behind me wrapping his arms around my frame.

Don't lie. Mehkai could smell a lie." I don't like when they throw her name around," I admitted looking up at a street light.

"Whose?"

"Frankee's...my mother's."

"Mmm..." He kissed my neck.

"They talk about her like what she did wasn't wrong. Include her in our family holiday memories and she doesn't deserve it."

He held me tighter.

"All that damn therapy my dad paid for was useless. How was I supposed to heal with her constantly being a conversation piece?" I asked him like he could give me the answer I was searching for. I knew he couldn't.

"I don't know how you feel, Ma. My mother's been around all my life."

Ouch.

He continued. "I'm sorry you had to miss out and all the things only a mother can teach you." His comment tore through my heart.

She'd missed everything. My first crush, my first kiss, boyfriend, date...menstrual. She never finished teaching me how to cook. Bake a cake. Put makeup on. She'd missed my middle school, high school, and college graduations.

Mehkai sighed. "Don't dwell on that shit. Let that shit mold you into the woman you're becoming."

"You're right," I mumbled.

"All you can do is be a better mother to our shorties when we have 'em." He shrugged.

I grinned. "You want me to have your *shorties*?" That New York slang was still funny to me.

"Of course...eventually."

"How you know I want to have your shorties?"

"Because." He placed his lips on my ear. "You catch 'em every time."

Even though it was freezing outside, I melted in his big arms. Just nasty. But I loved it. I loved *him*. The nigga from my hit list.

He wasn't lying. Protected sex hadn't been practiced between us. We'd strap up every once in a while, but for the most part we'd be skin to skin. My panties got wet just thinking about it.

"You're so nasty."

"I know." He kissed the side of my face.

***

"Uno out!" I yelled slamming my last card down on the pile. Thanks to Mehkai who made the color for us to play off yellow. He thought he was slick. This was the third time he'd done that. Each time resulting in me a win.

"Again!" Eve rolled her eyes. "Y'all cheating."

"Don't hate." I grabbed all the cards in the deck to shuffle them.

"I'm finished." Nisha slid her chair away from the table.

"Me too."

"Me too." One by one, everybody started slowly backing out of the game.

Sore losers. Kai's phone went off...again. And *again*, he ignored it, placing it back in his pocket. *What the hell was that about?*

"I see Blaze still cheats in Uno." My dad walked into the dining room passing Mehkai another Corona.

"She sure does." Uncle Monty cosigned.

"Viola, get the door!" My dad yelled.

"Don't no man, other than *me*, tell my wife to get anything." Uncle Monty frowned. "Vi, get your ass up and get the door. I know you hear it."

Everybody at the table burst into a fit of laughter. Well, except Mehkai. He was too engrossed in his phone. Texting. He looked up at me and then looked back down at his phone when it rang. Again, he ignored it.

Who the fuck is that?

I told Mehkai I wouldn't fight over him again, and I lied. I would go to war with my own father over Mehkai. I glanced over at his phone to see someone texted him kissing emojis. Then they texted him again, this time with heart eyes. He didn't reply. He just exited out of their messages.

His eyes met mine again. His saying, *"Don't start."* Mine screamed, *"Don't get you and that bitch fucked up."*

"Family!" I heard a familiar voice echo throughout the house before its owner reached the room.

I jumped up from my seat and looked over at my dad. He simply walked into the kitchen avoiding eye contact. Uncle Monty cleared his throat awkwardly, and everybody else looked toward the entrance.

Aunt Vi cut the corner first, smiling from ear to ear. "Look everybody." Her eyes landed on mine. Apologizing. "Look who came to see us."

The person behind her emerged, and the world became still. Our eyes connected. For the first time in fourteen years. I let mine roam over her, noticing she'd gained weight, but it looked good on her. She looked happy, like she'd been happy. Like the years without me had done her some justice. Made her better.

Her pixie haircut was fresh. The makeup on her face looked skillfully done. Her emerald eyes danced around me, reminding me a long time ago I'd wanted those same eyes. She was dressed in a tan pencil skirt, silk button blouse that was tucked in, and on her feet brown, leather deep V ankle booties. Her fashion sense always intact. At least *some* things hadn't changed. But she had.

I could tell by the way she looked at me. Like I was a stranger. Like she hadn't taught me how to ride a bike without training wheels or tie my shoe strings using the bunny ear method.

"Auntie Frankee!" Nisha jumped up from her chair, dashing toward her.

to be continued...

Made in United States
Orlando, FL
03 March 2024

44329492R00134